For Jayne +
with love

Joan.

27 October 1986.

Tentacles of Unreason

A list of the books in the series appears at the end of this volume.

TENTACLES OF UNREASON

Stories by
Joan Givner

UNIVERSITY OF ILLINOIS PRESS

Urbana and Chicago

*Publication of this work was supported in part
by grants from the National Endowment for the Arts
and the Illinois Arts Council, a state agency.*

©1985 by Joan Givner
Manufactured in the United States of America
C 5 4 3 2 1

This book is printed on acid-free paper.

Special thanks to *Ascent,* which published "The Decline and Fall of a
Reasonable Woman" and "First Love," to *North American Review,* which
published "A Spectator Sport," and to *Wascana Review,* which published
"The Lost Sheep."

Library of Congress Cataloging in Publication Data

Givner, Joan, 1936–
    Tentacles of unreason.

    (Illinois short fiction)
    I. Title.   II. Series.
PS3557.I86T4   1985   813'.54   84-24154
ISBN 0-252-01203-8 (alk. paper)

For Emily and Jessie

Contents

First Love

Whatever happened, it happened in a climate of extremes, and the winter of 1970 was the bitterest of them all. For months on end Victoria-la-Prairie was like a city under siege. Domes of arctic air clamped down and snuffed out everything necessary to human existence. The lake in the park froze to its very bed, and the wind whipped the flags on the legislative building tight around the flagpoles and held them, raised and stiff as javelins.

All movement was arrested. The runways at the airport were iced in, flights were canceled, and intercourse with the outside world cut off. Cars in the university parking lot refused to start and remained welded to the spot by ice and snow, like monuments sculpted in steel.

Sibyl, this year of all years, felt more isolated than ever, for during the construction of the new arts building, the faculty was housed in temporary quarters. She had been unaccountably separated from her colleagues in Philosophy and marooned in the midst of the English Department.

Her discomfort was not caused by the unfriendliness of her new neighbors. Far from it. They went out of their way, in fact, to make her feel at home, including her in conversations in the coffee lounge and inviting her to departmental gatherings. But close contact with them simply aggravated her sense of separateness and made her keenly aware that she did not speak their language. She was astounded by their disregard for the ordinary conventions of discourse. Amphibolies abounded in their conversation, non sequiturs went quite unnoticed, arguments-post-hoc-ergo-propter-hoc were accepted without censure, and questions were begged by the hour. All this, Sibyl concluded, came of constantly reading stories and poems and demonstrated what happened to intellects uncurbed by the discipline of Philosophy. Sometimes, as she strode the corridors, fragments of so-called lectures floated out of open doors, and she heard voices charged with emotion:

> Bright star, would I were steadfast as thou art

> I love thee to the depth and breadth and height
> My soul can reach

These scraps induced in Sibyl a faint sense of nausea, giving way first to pity and then to alarm as she imagined the effect of such flabbiness on the undergraduates. No wonder she, Sibyl, had such difficulty teaching them the art of thinking in general and the discipline of formal logic in particular. It seemed to her that these people were out of contact with what was ordinarily considered to be reality. Since her whole study was the nature of that reality, it shocked her to think of others fleeing from it so recklessly.

She began to study the English Department with an almost morbid fascination. She observed two main components. One group was English, drawn from the generation like herself of single children that grew up during World War II. They might have been the boy next door, for she felt she had known them all her life. Their fathers had been "called up" shortly after their sons' conceptions, and it had been left to their mothers to oversee their induction into the world. The mothers had named them Beverly, Robin, and Basil, but called them by pet names — Binky, Bobbin, and Bunny — and had raised them tenderly, warming their slippers in the hearth, tucking them snugly into their beds with hot water bottles, teddy bears, and tales of Beatrix Potter. When the soldiers returned they were appalled by what they found — called them Laddie, Sonny, and Boy, cropped off their ringlets, and started taking them to Rugby games. Alas, too late. They were mollycoddled beyond all possibility of recall. The fathers had cause to reflect that the casualties of war are not limited to the battlefield. And finally, they had to admit that their sons were not bad lads. They warbled tunefully in church choirs, worked hard at their studies, and were kind to old ladies and small dogs. They won scholarships to the grammar school and later open scholarships to the university. Once there, they caused little apprehension. There were no wild pranks like setting fire to taxis, placing bombs in letter boxes, and demanding Home Rule for Wales. Blamelessly they sang in college glee clubs and madrigal groups. They were still doing so, and it gave Sibyl a twinge of nostalgia to hear their voices floating down the halls:

> Whoso by foolish love are stung are worthily distressed
> And so sing I, with a down a down a down
>
> None but I this lip must owe,
> Hey nonny, nonny no!

They sang melodiously, passionately, as if only in song and verse could they pour out their hearts.

The other component of the English Department was quite foreign to Sibyl. The members of this group came from universities in the Middle West with strange names (though not, she presumed, unaccredited) like Terre Haute State Teachers College, Ball State, and Purdue. She noted that the graduates of these institutions seemed to be constantly undergoing some kind of ideological identity crisis. This was reflected in their rapidly changing appearances. When they first came for job interviews, they had been called Alwyn, Arthur, and Irving, had been clean-shaven, gray-flanneled, and accompanied by neat little wives. But after they were hired, they reported for duty as Al, Art, and Irv, bearded and blue-jeaned, and accompanied by other people's wives. Nor did the transformation stop there, but eventually gave way to other manifestations. Currently a wave of Sino-philia had them all in pyjamalike uniforms in drab colors. For a whimsical touch they had adopted the headgear of artisans of other nations—the gorblimey hats of London dustmen, berets from the Basque region of Spain, or the caps of Greek fishermen. The wives had now departed and their places were taken by female students. It was all very well, Sibyl thought, to be wearing the uniform of an idea, but they carried everything to excess.

Yet tolerance was necessary, for it was clear that Sibyl would spend the rest of her life with these people. There had been a time when they all moved around merrily as in a great academic game of musical chairs, doing two-year stints here and there. Suddenly, however, the music had stopped. The baby boom had ended, enrollments dropped, funds dried up, the bottom fell out of the job market, and there they were. For Sibyl and her mismatched colleagues, it happened to be in the middle of the Canadian Plains. Already now they had been there for ten years. They were middle-aged and moving in a body toward old age, senior citizenship, and senility. They would buy soapstone carvings for each other on retirement, present them at testimonial dinners, and they would shudder to ask for whom the university flag was lowered to half mast.

Sibyl tried to accept her colleagues as she hoped they accepted her. She was forty-five years old, chaste, lantern-jawed, and extremely myopic, a weakness which she corrected by wearing glasses with strong lenses. She was argumentative but not contentious, somewhat quick to an opinion but not opinionated. She felt that her greatest asset was her clear-eyed, no-nonsense way of looking at the world. A former professor had once described her as a "brisk thinker." And so she felt confident she was until her displacement brought her into close contact with the English Department and their unsettling manners.

The English Department open houses dramatized her problems of relating to these people. One group in sock feet huddled around someone with a pitch pipe singing round songs, part songs, patter songs from Gilbert and Sullivan, and madrigals:

The flowers that bloom in the spring tra la la

Oh Sir Jasper do not touch me

They called out in a friendly way to Sibyl, "Come and join us, darling, we need a soprano." But Sibyl had a rich contralto voice and besides she didn't know the words.

"Well, hum, darling, hum," they said, but Sibyl preferred to talk.

She went to find the others, who, bypassing the rum-based punch set out for general consumption, were engaged in a treasure hunt for the host's serious liquor. Soon they located it in the linen closet, the grandfather clock, or the medicine chest, and once fortified with it, they made lecherous advances to the women present and even to Sibyl herself. When she asked a Ukrainian colleague in a conversational way if he wrote Easter eggs, he winked boldly and said, "No, I lay them. Are you a Ukrainian Easter egg, Sibyl?"

She moved on rather fast and told another person about a paper she was working on. But when she paused to inquire if she was boring him, he said, leering at her, "Only when you talk, old girl."

Alarmed, she moved to where the faculty wives were herded together in one end of the room. She asked about the children and they replied with the creeds and manifestoes of their husbands. "Dunc believes . . ." "Dunc feels . . ." "Dunc's convinced. . . ." She thought the women were mouthpieces for the oracular wisdom of invisible deities, and that she, Sibyl, was carrying on conversation by proxy with their emissaries.

When she approached the deities themselves, she found them by now thick-tongued, fumey-breathed, and not oracular at all: "Shibble, Shibble. Wassa nice girl like you doing living alone? Shouldn't be allowed. Mosh horrable. . . ."

So was the alternative, Sibyl thought, looking around before she went off to drag her coat from under the couple who were rolling about on the bed in the master bedroom.

Life might well have continued in this way, not exactly smoothly but without upheaval, with everyone tolerating everyone else's weaknesses. But the climate was against it. The winter in its savagery pushed people to extreme postures. February was the fatal month. Housewives got cabin fever, marriages collapsed, and the rate of changing partners accelerated alarmingly. Whole departments rose against their chairmen, chairmen battled with assistant deans, and deans warred with the vice-president. People began to drink to excess. Those previously doing so turned to drugs. Those already on drugs took overdoses, got rushed to the emergency room, and collections had to be taken up for bouquets of flowers.

Throughout all this, Sibyl worked away single-mindedly at a philosophical problem which she intended to present later in the year at one of the big international Philosophical Association meetings. In order to prepare herself, she intended to read an early version to the

History of Science seminar, which was the main forum of intellectual
activity in the university. The seminars took place every Thursday
evening, and Sibyl's presentation was scheduled for the second
Thursday of the month between a paper on cooperative learning in
China and one on skipping songs by a member of the English Department, who liked folklore or children or both and was a tireless
researcher in the playgrounds of the local schools. Sibyl's paper was
a *Gedankenexperiment,* a thought experiment. It was somewhat
technical but she had tried, by using an imaginative image, to make
it appealing and understandable to the layperson.

The procedure at the meetings was that the paper was read, the
chairman of the meeting offered his commentary, and then, while
drinks were served, the paper was open to general discussion. The
schedule was so tight that canceled meetings could not be made up.
In this case, the paper was circulated in written form and comments
were invited. But few people bothered to read the papers and even
fewer to respond. It was a great blow, therefore, that the evening on
which Sibyl was scheduled to give her paper saw the most devastating
storm of the year. The temperature plummeted to forty below. The
windchill factor sent it even lower. Blowing snow reduced the visi-
bility to nil, and all traffic stopped completely. The students had to
cancel their Valentine Dance. Professors having one for the road in
the faculty club never reached the road at all. And there was no question of anyone's driving across town to attend the seminar.

Disconsolately, Sibyl walked over from the residence where she
had rooms to the English Department lounge, thinking that if only
one or two people were there she might still read her paper. But the
three who had been stranded by the storm were already beyond the
point of rational discourse. Dunc was acting as bartender. The other
two were natives of Saskatchewan, and they were already showing
that curious excitement that blizzards arouse in prairie-dwellers and
Siberian huskies. They were sniffing the air happily and feeding their
regional pride by topping each other's remembrances of blizzards
past:

On such a night as this
. . . grandfather's false teeth frozen solid in the milk pail. . . .

On such a night

. . . there was a dog frozen stiff as stiff. . . .

. . . there was grandmother frozen to the outhouse seat. . . .

Duncan gave Sibyl a very generous tumbler full of amber liquid. Since she had not eaten dinner and had a low tolerance for alcohol anyway, the drink immediately induced in her a sensation of dizziness. Shapes and colors became blurred, and she retreated at once into a private bubble of her own. It was far from unpleasant. Outside, the wind howled alarmingly. Somewhere inside the building the Elizabethan singers were harmonizing and she caught fragments of their songs:

> Unkind, oh, stay thy flying
>
> Oft have I sighed for him that hears me not

At her elbow Duncan was explaining a surefire technique for avoiding a hangover. The room was dim and smokey and she felt herself floating in a vague misty haze.

It was in this slightly disembodied state that Sibyl distinguished a person standing in the doorway. When she concentrated hard, she could see that it was the figure of a man leaning against the door frame. He was dark with very bright eyes and was in sock feet, one foot raised and rubbing the ankle of the other leg. It was Sam Werner, a member of the English Department, who kept to himself so completely that Sibyl could never remember having spoken to him at all. He seemed to be making a signal with his eyebrow, and when she looked carefully, Sibyl saw that he was beckoning to her. Carrying her drink very carefully so as not to spill it, she went over to see what he wanted.

"Don't let Dunc give you that stuff," he said. "You'll get a terrific hangover and not be able to teach tomorrow."

"Oh, but you see," Sibyl explained, "Dunc was just telling me precisely how to avoid a hangover. That was what he was telling me just now."

"There's only one way to do that," Sam Werner said, and taking her drink, he sniffed at it suspiciously. Then, holding her by the elbow, he guided her into his office. Sibyl had never been there before, and she found it astonishingly unlike an office. There was a white bear rug on the floor, a pot of white hyacinths blooming on the desk, an armchair with cushions, and a tray with bottles and glasses and a refillable soda siphon. He had obviously been working because his typewriter was uncovered and purring. He switched it off, emptied Sibyl's drink into the hyacinths, and handed her another one as she sat in the armchair.

"Too bad about your paper," he said. "It sounded interesting. Tell me about it."

"Well, I'm interested in sense data and the nature of perception," she told him, but very tentatively because most people found her work boring. . . .

"Go on," he said.

"I've postulated a sentient windsock. . . ."

"You've postulated a what?"

"A windsock, just the ordinary kind you see at the airport, only this one has a sentient organ. The only thing it can sense is the wind. Imagine a windsock with cloth as sensitive as skin, can you?"

"I'm trying," he said, narrowing his eyes.

"The thing is that the windsock is also a means of indicating to others the presence of wind. So there are two questions. How do you sense the presence of wind, and how does the windsock sense the wind? Well, it senses the presence when the air fills and expands it. It senses the absence of air when it hangs limp, do you see?"

"I'm beginning to," he said.

"Imagine," she continued, "how the windsock would think of wind. Not as something that stirs the trees or rustles the waves, but simply as something that enters and expands and inflates itself. It could never separate its own idea of wind from the general idea. And its own understanding of wind and air would be quite different from what it indicates about them to others. Can you understand that?"

"Yes, I can," he said, "and I'm glad you explained it to me alone. It would have been quite wasted on Dunc and the others."

He was perched on the edge of his desk, and when he suggested that Sibyl kick off her shoes and stretch out on the rug, it seemed like an infinitely reasonable suggestion.

"No question of leaving the building tonight," he said, settling cushions behind her head and setting her drink on the table.

"But I just live in College West," she said.

"Well, anyway," he said, "you might not make it past the wild rout out there."

It did, indeed, seem to be getting very noisy in the lounge. At one point Dunc pounded on the office door and shouted, "Release that woman," but they didn't answer and he went off singing, "Hello, young lovers wherever you are." They heard him lurching clumsily along the corridor.

Outside, the blizzard raged louder than ever. On the floor above, the Elizabethan singers were harmonizing sweetly, and at the end of the hall Dunc and his friends were roaring and shouting. Sam Werner stretched out beside Sibyl and told her, "That was very heady stuff, all that about the windsock and its sentient organ," and he switched off the light.

When Sibyl opened her eyes, the storm had spent itself completely and the morning sun was shining blindingly through the windows and curtains. As she adjusted to the brightness, she saw that she was lying on the bear rug under a light cover. Beside her on the floor, completely uncovered and unclothed, lay Sam Werner with his eyes closed and a smile on his face. Since she had not, so far as she could remember, seen a naked man so close, she put on her glasses and looked at him intently. He was like a satyr, covered with black hair to the tops of his thighs and on his arms and chest. Having so much hair, he did not appear, even without clothes, to be naked, and Sibyl was just thinking what an agreeable sight he was, when the bell in the corridor rang out very loud.

"You've got an eight-thirty class," Sam Werner said without opening his eyes. "I put your clothes in the filing cabinet."

"I don't think that's the eight o'clock bell," she said. "I expect the storm affected the wires and it's rung too early."

She felt very disinclined to move because the sun was warm, the bear rug was soft, and she liked looking at Sam Werner.

"You bet it's eight o'clock," he said. "The cleaners will be in soon, and you'd better get off to class."

"I don't expect there'll be any students," she said. "They'll all be digging out."

It was a day for digging out and clearing away the debris and disorder caused by the storm. When she did finally get dressed and walk down the hall, she found Borden Boychuck stretched out on a sofa in the lounge, snoring very loudly. When she stepped into the elevator, she was joined by two of the madrigal singers. They were wearing matching parkas with pointed fur hoods, and they looked like miniature Christmas tree Santas, one red and one white. They waggled their fingers at her happily and said, "Did you have a lovely blizzard, darling? We did." When they stepped out of the elevator on the ground floor of the library, they found Dunc trying to look something up in the card catalogue. His hair was all on end, he was breathing heavily, and he was wearing a pair of slightly soiled long-johns, over which he had neglected to put on his trousers. The librarians were huddled together watching him very nervously.

"Oh my oh my! That Duncan, the naughty thing," the madrigal singers said. "No trousies on and frightening ladies. Shame on him." Deftly switching their purses to the other shoulder, each took one of his arms and steered him toward the elevator.

Sibyl went off to her class feeling very lighthearted and full of goodwill to all men. She stood at the podium and beamed at the few sleepy students scattered about the large lecture room. She started to talk about the *Symposium* and managed to get through without once having to refer to her notes. She could never remember finding the *Symposium* so delightful and lecturing on it so fluently. The storm seemed to have cleared her mind and freshened her senses and left her vibrant and alert.

"Why am I so changed?" she asked herself.

All day she caught glimpses of Sam Werner. Once she went by the open door of a classroom in which he was lecturing on Chaucer. He waved at her but didn't interrupt the flow of his lecture. Later she saw him in the hall laughing with a student who had long blond hair and a very short skirt. Sibyl hated the student and wished she was dead and then felt rather shocked at herself. Still later she saw him reading the newspapers in the library, but he did not look up when she passed. She began to feel a certain anxiety that the day would slip away and she would not talk to him. Finally at four-thirty she broke down and knocked at the door of his office. He stopped typing and said, "I was just about to come and look for you."

"Were you?" she said, delighted. "I thought you might like to come and have a drink with me."

He did like to, but when he entered her rooms, he said, "Good god, Sibyl, what a mess! How can you live like this?"

She was somewhat abashed by his reaction, but not surprised. It was a simple fact that although she was very organized in her work, she could not impose the same order on her surroundings. She could never bring herself to throw out newspapers and magazines lest she lose some vital information. Her filing system for mail broke down when people for whom she had no slot sent letters, and these tended to gather in large piles on tables and chairs. She was also extremely careless about replacing books once she had taken them down from the shelves. But she told herself that it was better to have a disorderly room than a disorderly mind.

"What were you going to have for dinner?" he asked.

"One of those frozen dinners," she said, adding hopefully that she had an extra one.

It did not seem to appeal to him and he said at last, "Look here, Sibyl, I think you'd better move in with me for a bit and raise your standard of living. But you'll be on probation, mind. You simply must learn to throw out newspapers, put books back on the shelves and pick up your clothes. Promise?"

She promised. And so Sibyl started to live with Sam Werner, and indeed her standard of living rose dramatically. No more frozen dinners, no more instant coffee, no more cheap wine in gallon jugs. He was very domestic and showed her how to do things properly.

"You've been living like an insect," he said, and she began to see that this was so.

She learned how to pick out steaks with white veins running through them and to tell the difference between the well-marbled and the well-gristled. She learned to cook them by searing them quickly and then adding butter and garlic and wine to make a rich sauce. They did this in the evenings and sat in the candlelight, mopping up the sauce with lumps of bread. Then they talked about the wine, how it smelled, tasted, and compared with the wine they had the day before, for Sibyl no longer drank it down thoughtlessly as if it were pop.

Once, she asked him, marveling, "Why is it that you didn't marry?"

"I got news for you," he said, and showed her photographs of two groups of children. "I've been burned not once but twice."

"Didn't they like having their standards of living raised?" Sibyl asked in astonishment.

"Apparently they did. But they eventually went off to raise someone else's."

So Sibyl asked no more, but she remembered all these things in her heart.

She was no longer working on her sentient windsock paper because she preferred to relax in the evenings. They cooked, listened to music, read, talked and went to bed. Sam Werner was working on the bilingual pun in Chaucer, and Sibyl was reading *Troilus and Criseyda* and "The Miller's Tale" and "The Reeve's Tale." He showed her what was funny and explained the jokes. He was reading Plato and she was explaining the arguments to him.

"Lie down with philosophers and you get up with ideas," Sam Werner said.

Thus, comfortably, February slipped away and March and April. At last winter relaxed its grip on the prairies. The Lenten season passed, the snow melted, and the academic year drew to a close. In other places flowers bloomed, the sap rose again, and the air softened, but on the central plains spring is often lost in the quick transition from cold to heat. Yet Sibyl sensed that it was spring. If someone had blindfolded and handcuffed her and rolled her out on to the prairie, she would have known the season from the sticky texture of the gumbo soil.

Usually at this time of year she planned her annual pilgrimage to visit her parents, but this year she had lost all interest in going home. She felt at home where she was and thought that her only ambition for the summer was to make a garden. One night before she switched off her reading lamp, she thought of this and resolved to mention it the next day to Sam Werner.

At breakfast she said, "I've been thinking. We should get some topsoil and make a vegetable garden in the back. We could grow all sorts of things — tomatoes, lettuce, onions. We might even think of an asparagus bed, though we wouldn't get any asparagus this year. . . ."

"Look, Sibyl," he said, "I've been thinking too. We can't go on like this forever, you know. For one thing, I'm going away next year."

"But where?" she said. "And why?"

"Why?" he said. "Why not? I have a sabbatical coming up and I'm off to Cambridge to use the Widener."

"But you'll be back at the end of the year, won't you?"

"I certainly hope not. Look, Sibyl, I'm a New Yorker by birth, and Victoria-la-Prairie is not my natural habitat. Not by a very long shot. I intend to do some serious job-hunting next year and never, if I can help it, return to this ungodly climate."

"But you said you worked well here."

"Well, that's true to a certain extent," he said. "But I'm not about to push my luck. You've seen what happens to people here. When they first arrive they're perfectly respectable scholars. Look at them in a few years and what do you find? First they're submitting papers to nonrefereed journals. Then they're sending in notes and reviews and then nothing at all. Next thing you hear they're raising pigs in Pense or breeding Siberian Huskies in Pilot Butte. I intend to get out before it's too late."

"But what about me?"

"Sibyl, listen. You're a perfectly wonderful girl and intelligent too. . . ."

"But I'm not a girl is that it? And I'm not pretty and I have too many bad habits?"

"That is not it at all. I'm not young myself. And you don't have nearly as many bad habits as you used to have, and the ones you do have I've gotten used to. In fact, I shall miss them. But I do not intend to live with anyone permanently. I've been married twice already. I'm paying alimony to one wife and child support to two. I have bought this house twice, once when I moved here and once after the divorce settlement. I have no intention of getting involved ever again in a so-called permanent relationship. In other words, I've no intention of getting married."

Sibyl was prepared to argue the point, but Sam Werner held up his right hand like a traffic policeman to silence her.

"Sibyl," he said, "you're an excellent philosopher, but you have to realize that there are some situations that cannot be resolved by argument."

And finally, realizing this was so, Sibyl admitted defeat. She moved back to her old rooms in the college residence, took up once more her sentient windsock paper, and tried to find consolation in Philosophy. But it was not easy for her to resume her former life. She was conscious now of an emptiness she had never noticed before. She found herself despising her solitary meals, her cramped apartment. The very silence and solitude which at one time she had cherished now oppressed her. When she met married couples and pairs of friends, instead of feeling superior, she looked at them wistfully. And she found herself taking an excessive interest in the new appointments in the English Department. She dreamed that the new appointment in linguistics, intended as Sam Werner's replacement, would be a man of a certain age, unmarried and needing to have his standard of living raised.

Alas, her prayers were unanswered. The search committee searched long and hard, and finally in its wisdom appointed a jaunty young woman from Bryn Mawr with a halo of frizzled hair. She strode about the halls in a pant suit and talked of offering a course in Women's Studies. After the initial disappointment, however, Sibyl had to admit that Genevieve was bright and original and brilliant in conversation. She hoped that they might become friends.

At one open house in the middle of the next winter, the two of them stood together by the fire chatting. Genevieve looked stunning in a black velvet jacket, a white blouse with ruffles up the front, black trousers and shiny leather boots. The rings on her fingers caught the firelight and sparkled. Her green eyes, as she talked, flashed in the startling pallor of her face and darted about the room with amused and secretive glances. She reminded Sibyl of a mezzotint of Colette.

"Do you like Mexican food?" she asked, and Sibyl said she didn't know and that she didn't cook much herself any more since she was living alone at the present. . . ."

"Yeah," Genevieve said. "They told me you'd been living with some dude."

"Some dude?" Sibyl said. "That was Sam Werner, your predecessor. . . ."

"My predecessor, was he?" Genevieve said. "Well, well," and dusting the room with her bright eyes she said, "These creeps. . . ."

In the hallway various people were holding up Dunc while others were trying to put on his boots, and someone was saying, "Did he have a hat, does anyone know?"

Dunc himself, instead of cooperating, was giving an operatic rendering of a popular song. He hailed Sibyl and then continued:

> "I'm starry-eyed and vaguely discontented
> Like a nightingale without a song to sing
> Yet I feel so gay in a melancholy way
> That it might as well be spring. . . ."

Finally they found his scattered garments, dressed him up, and steered him out the door. Sibyl followed. It was a bright moonlight night with a sky full of stars and hoarfrost twinkling on the branches of the trees. Dunc twirled about in the driveway caroling, "I haven't seen a crocus or a rosebud."

"Want a ride home, Sibyl?" someone called. "We're going your way." But it was a soft winter night and Sibyl preferred to walk. She set off walking briskly down the street. As she turned the corner she could still hear Dunc's voice in the distance,

> "I'm as jumpy as a puppet on a string
> I'd say that I had spring fever. . . ."

Crossing the street, she entered the park and paused at the entrance to one of the tree-encircled meadows. It was so peaceful there that she stepped inside on the untrodden snow and sat on the low branch of a tree looking about her. The moon and stars shone overhead and everything was white and sparkling and still. It was like a stage set for *Swan Lake,* and she expected at any moment to see leaping from the wings a charming effeminate Siegfried.

And, indeed, just as she thought so, a figure did stride out from the shadows. It was not a dazzling white prince, however, but Genevieve in a dark cloak like a great black swan.

"Genevieve," she gasped. "You!"

"Sibyl," Genevieve mocked. "You!" And she unfurled her cloak and lifted her arms and spread them wide in a generous gesture of welcome.

"Sibyl," she said, "come home with me and I will show you delights you never dreamed of."

"Oh, my goodness," Sibyl said, rather shocked.

But Genevieve smiled her brilliant darting smile and wrapped Sibyl about with the great capacious cloak and put her arm about Sibyl's waist. All across the park, two pairs of footprints twined and merged as they tracked together over the virgin snow.

Brains

Sophie Lewty never thought about brains. At least not for the first ten years of her life. Then for the next ten years, she thought about them all the time. It started when she took the 11-plus exams.

Altogether, Sophie took three sets of exams. She took the one for the local grammar school at the elementary school in the next village. It lasted all day, and when there was a break, her mother appeared in the playground with a thermos of hot tea, heavily laced with sugar as recommended for cases of shock.

For the Manchester High School exam they had to go to town by train. The examination room was a great vaulted hall filled with dark, foreign-looking girls. The test was hard. They were asked to divide sentences into subject and predicate, but Sophie had not taken that in school, so she had to guess a great deal. At noon they were given an hour break, and Sophie and her mother went to a Kardomah cafe and had baked beans on toast.

"How d'you think you did?" asked her mother.

"I did alright," said Sophie, but only to avoid questions. She was far from confident.

At the Bolton School, since there was an interview as well as a written exam, they had to go into Bolton twice in one week, traveling by tram, trolley, and bus. It was quite exhausting. Her parents coached her a bit for the interview, advising her, "If they ask what your father does, don't say he's a clerk, say he's a compensation officer. And try to get in that you write poetry."

When she brought up the poetry, one of the teachers asked which she found more difficult, the rhyme or the rhythm. She had never consciously thought of either and had not even heard of rhythm.

When the results were published, Sophie had failed the Manchester High School for Girls, and had failed the Bolton School but had been placed on a waiting list in case of cancellations. She was accepted for Leigh Grammar School, but her entrance was deferred for one year. There was much discussion at home about what the deferral meant. Was she not sufficiently clever for immediate admittance, or was it simply a question of when her birthday fell?

After a few weeks she heard that there was a place for her at the Bolton School, and she accepted it, thus beginning several years of daily two-hour journeys by tram, trolley, and bus. After a time Lancashire United modernized its transportation system. Trams and trolleys were declared obsolete and replaced entirely by buses. The journey, however, took just as long after this advance as before.

At the end of the first year, 25 girls from the 100 admitted were put into a special class for those destined for the university. They were to do more advanced math and French and take extra subjects like Latin, which were required for university entrance. Sophie was one of the ones chosen, and her parents were ecstatic. Her father said, "I told you all along there was nothing wrong with the kid's brains." This was Sophie's first inkling that the effectiveness of her brains had been called into question, and she was filled with a profound sense of uneasiness.

She was approaching adolescence and supposedly prey to all the anxieties attendant on this period of emotional and physical dislocation. But such worries were entirely submerged in the greater waves of self-doubt that swept over her when she thought about her brains.

That she should have been so troubled was the result of various circumstances, among them her mother's exaggerated dynastic sense. This manifested itself in a tendency to trace the most trivial personal mannerisms and dietary preferences to some ancestral source. Thus, whenever Sophie's fondness for rich desserts and creamy foods became evident—as it often did—her mother remarked with the regularity of a tic, "Sophie Lewty, I could swear you take after your Grandfather Lewty. You've got his sweet tooth. Nobody on my side ever had such a sweet tooth." If she had a craving for kippers, her mother pounced on the appetite with a surge of family pride, "You're just like my father. He used to say he'd give his eyeteeth for a good kipper, and my mother couldn't even abide them cooking in the house."

These genetic theories were reinforced by neighbors who told her, "You didn't get that red hair from your mum and dad, Sophie Lewty." When she tried to ascertain the source of her hair, her mother was contemptuous. "Why, there's red hair on both sides. My cousin Herbert Laithwaite was very sandy before he went gray. And what about your dad's great-aunt Ginger Glegg?"

As a consequence, Sophie knew herself to be a ragbag of hand-me-down genes from various relatives, but mainly from her grandparents. Common sense might have canceled out this knowledge, but working against it was the constant repetition which reinforced her mother's theories. Sophie was often drawn into a ritual of question and response.

"I've never come across a sweet tooth to match yours, Sophie Lewty."

"Well, I get it from me Grandad Lewty."

"Where else could you get it from?"

"Not from your side, Mum."

What chance did clear daylight reason have against the weight of popular opinion and the authority of conditioned response? And quite naturally, once the precept was established, she sought the source of her brain cells. Once she did that, her prospects began to look very gloomy indeed.

She had little to go on in the case of her grandfathers since they were both dead. But even their absence seemed sinister — the feeble disinclination of the unfit to survive. On the other hand, the image of her grandmothers brought her near to panic, for they were both definitely odd. Her mother, in fact, referred to them as if they belonged to a subhuman species.

Sophie realized, of course, that they were not in the same category as the certifiable mental cases, of which there were a fair number in the village. A girl in the same class had two elderly relatives who sat by the kitchen fire all day vacuously dreaming and drooling. At first Sophie found them alarming, but Elsie Roley told her, "That's just me Uncle Freddy and Aunt Lil. They're not all there," and Sophie eventually accepted them as fixtures by the hearth, harmless and in-articulate like the great mastiffs that panted beside them.

Nor indeed were her own grandmothers extreme cases of public and ludicrous oddity like the old women who wore men's shoes and went grocery shopping with decrepit prams. These provided the sub-stance of village gossip and amusement until the day they finally dis-appeared, leaving behind the terse explanatory epitaph: "They came and took her away."

Yet, while the grandmothers did not fall into these extreme cate-gories, they were clearly peculiar, not entirely all there. They lived in big airless houses, rarely went out, and dressed in outlandish clothes — depilated fur coats, straw hats and shawls — whatever came to hand and was convenient for keeping out drafts, holding tendrils of hair in check, or accommodating misshapen feet. They slept and ate all hours of the day and night.

"I've only myself to please, so I eat just when it suits me," they both said. Her Grandmother Watson made stews, hashes, and hot-pots, meat and vegetables all simmering together in one large cast-iron crock until they were reduced to the same unvarying flavor. Her Grandmother Lewty cooked paired items on the top of the stove, hovering over them with burning cheeks, prodding and goading them — sausage and mash, liver and bacon, tripe and onions, dishes that gave off wonderful smells that lingered in upholstery and clothes and made visitors feel famished.

Willing neighbors and relatives ran in and out doing odd jobs and errands for the grandmothers, but of all these Sophie was the most indispensable, qualified by specialized talents. She had a natural facility for memorizing the prices of food and other commodities, and always got the best bargains. Moreover, she had a great capacity for following instructions both explicit and implicit.

For her Grandmother Lewty she brought reading material. Any-one could have taken a list to the public library, but only Sophie de-veloped an instinct for the books of a vaguely disreputable kind that pleased her grandmother. She picked out the books, now by the titles and now by the pictures on the jackets, brought them home discreet-ly, and placed them where they would not be turned up by those dusting and vacuuming. She chose *East Lynn, Forever Amber,* and *No Orchards for Miss Blandish,* and mentioned to her mother that her Granny Lewty liked reading "The Classics."

If her Grandmother Watson said to Sophie's mother, "Tell Freddy Betts that fish was off," her mother replied, "I'll do nothing of the kind. If you have any complaints you'll tell him yourself." But Sophie seized the chance to be rude without responsibility. She couldn't get fast enough to the crowded shop to stand in front of the counter and pipe up, "My grandmother said that piece of plaice was off. Even the cat next door wouldn't look at it, and we couldn't get the smell out of the house for a week." Droll faces, semi-scandalized, turned on her, and the fishmonger said, "Chip off the old block, that one." Which block she never had the nerve to ask.

But Sophie valued her commissions for other benefits. The most tangible was that the tips they brought in provided her with an independent income. Above all, however, was the fact that her work gave her status. The grandmothers were the only two people in her world to whom she could feel securely superior and condescending, imbued as she was with her mother's conviction that they were foolish, ridiculous, and generally beyond the pale.

Her mother dispensed righteous indignation lavishly in all directions but on the grandmothers with particular generosity. Toward her husband's mother she felt the contempt of the virtuous woman for the hedonist.

"Cheerful, happy-go-lucky, never gives a thought to anyone else," she said.

"But she doesn't bother anybody much," said Sophie's father, "and at her age that's something."

"She was the same at any age," said her mother, her tone hinting at a long catalogue of remembered grudges.

Toward her own mother her attitude was more complicated, fraught with conflict, aggravated by similarities of temperament, long association, and differences of opinion. There was shame too, for the old woman was ignorant and illiterate, spoke badly, and understood all worldly matters imperfectly. Her use of language was really shocking, utterly independent of the rules of grammar and pronunciation. When she mentioned her own mother, Sophie's mother's brow furrowed deeply, and she pressed her hand against her forehead as if she felt a spasm of pain. The only person with whom she could discuss the old woman without embarrassment was her sister, Sophie's Aunt Fan. The two sisters liked to sit together over a pot of tea, Aunt Fan chain-smoking woodbines from the green packages that she crammed in her handbag. They whispered confidentially, like members of a hermetic cult, and Sophie lurking nearby heard the same muttered phrases,

"Wait till you hear the latest. . . ."

"Eh, what d'you think she told our Sophie the other day. . . ."

"Honestly, the nerve. . . ."

The areas of conflict between the old woman and her daughters were manifold. Chief among them was that the daughters had "got religion," a circumstance the old woman regarded as slightly more bizarre than if they had taken to cannibalism. She saw their churches as part of a great conspiracy to siphon off all her money and channel it to dubious purposes abroad—foreign missions, savages, and the Pope. Her daughter Fan had converted to Catholicism, while Betsy, Sophie's mother, was a devout member of the Church of England. These allegiances placed the old woman in a quandary, for she liked to dispense crackling pound notes to the daughters and jingling half-crowns to Sophie. Yet she feared always that the money would end up in the offertory box in some church and find its way thence to the pockets of vicar, priest, or foreigner. When she gave Sophie money, she cautioned her outright, "And *don't* give it to the church." To her daughters she said more guardedly, "And *don't* give it away."

Charity and piety, the twin virtues of Sophie's mother, were repugnant to the old woman, though she made donations regularly to the Injured Jockeys' Fund. She gave with the generosity of the power-hungry, the dispenser of largesse who exacts obligation in return. While the daughters knew this, they were not so well off that they could afford to turn up their noses at pound notes and fivers whatever the source—they spelled new shoes, a new hat, new upholstery for a threadbare chair—but they accepted grudgingly.

The grandmother had her own specialized vocation. At its highest, it took the form of juggling her investments, playing the stock-market, reading the financial times, buying shares and selling them.

At its lowest, it dwindled to doing competitions in the daily papers and the *News of the World,* filling out football coupons, and betting on horse races. She was always surrounded by the trappings of her calling — a sea of newsprint, stamps, envelopes, pens and pencils, and she rudely warned off interruptions when she was at work. "Hush up, you. Can't you see I'm doin' me cal-kill-ations." And she energetically scribbled, scrubbed out, and scribbled again, licking the pencil and making notations and marks all over the papers.

She tried to convert Sophie, telling her, "I'll buy you some shares. Look at this list and pick summat off it." Sophie studied the dull list of merchandise and chose arbitrarily, whatever began with an unusual letter — X, Y, or Z. Her grandmother sniffed at her choice, but sometimes, weeks later, she told Sophie, "Them Viyella shares you picked is doin' alright. They've been goin' up and up."

Before a horse race she told Sophie, "Pick a horse from that list and when Johnny Sefton goes out, he'll put ten bob on for you." Sophie studied the list and chose names that appealed to her — Churchtown Boy, Royal Runner, Never-Say-Die. . . . Her grandmother glared as if Sophie were lost beyond any possibility of reclamation. "What did you pick that one for? It's the favorite. Ten to one."

"I like the name, though."

"You've got to look at the odds, you gobbin. Now pick this 'ere, that's thirty-three to one. You've got to apply yourself. You can't go by the name."

"Well, I did with Viyella and that won."

"That was just *luck.*"

After the big races the grandmother always had money to give away. Sophie asked her mother, "how does she always win? How can she know?"

"She doesn't," said her mother. "There's only one way to keep winning. Use your noggin."

"Lucky?" said Sophie.

"Don't talk daft. She backs half the field. You back enough, and you're sure to come up on some. She must lose twice what she makes. I bet she could live in a detached house and be riding about in a car with what she spends on races."

"But why does she do it?"

"Well, she's a gambler. It's a disease. She can't help herself. It's the same with drinkers. They can't help theirselves."

Sophie checked that answer against the grandmother's.

"Why are you always studying the races and the stockmarket?" Her grandmother looked disgusted.

"You've got to watch your money. If you don't, you'll end up like your mother and your Aunt Fan. They never do nothin', and they never have anythin', and they never will. Not that it would do them much good if they had any. Give it to the church as like as not. Money thrown down the drain."

"Somebody has to support the church," said Sophie automatically.

"Oh they do, do they?" said the grandmother. "Well, not with my money they don't. You don't believe all that stuff they tell you in church, do you?"

"You know," said Sophie, "I don't. But don't let on to my mum."

When she left that day, her grandmother gave her a pound note.

"Hey, thanks," said Sophie. "Have you come up on something?"

"I did an' I didn't," said the grandmother.

Sophie's mother often asked in a sharp, nagging voice, "Why do you spend so much time with your Grandma Watson? Sitting there all Sunday afternoon. What do you do? Why don't you stick with friends your own age?" The question gave Sophie pause, for, in fact, she took little pleasure in the conversations of her school friends. They were preoccupied with school matters—getting on teams for netball, lacrosse, and tennis; winning matches; taking exams; speculating on the abilities of each other and the rest of the class—who was "brilliant," was merely "a swot," and who would "go far," winning county scholarships, state scholarships, open scholarships to Oxford and Cambridge and eventually get "Firsts."

Sophie had decided that she would like to go to the university if she were not nobbled by her ancestral intellectual baggage. Things had changed in the village since Sophie started to the Bolton School. When she first got her scholarship, many of the villagers had sneered, especially the abject hags from the jig who wore black shawls and clogs. They said it was a shame for girls to take the lads' places when all they would do was get married. And that educating women was a mug's game. Old Walter Rudd said, "You'll end up an old maid, like Fanny Lummux."

But slowly things were changing. It started with Len Simmonds, a man ever ahead of his time, the first to fly in the face of custom and have the first telephone installed, the first television, the first car that was not the traditional somber gray and black but bright red. He announced in the Red Lion one night that his daughter was going to college and that "he didn't want a penny back." This remark was circulated and subjected to various interpretations. In some quarters it was greeted with sheer disbelief, in others with derision, and in some with admiration. But what did it mean? Was he boasting that he could afford such a gesture of extravagance, or was there some hidden benefit in having a college-educated daughter? Long-established village custom had stipulated that girls who went to college returned home and turned their weekly paychecks over to the family until the debt was paid off. When it was, they had usually been "on the shelf" for a good ten years, and either remained at home or moved to their own house with another unmarried sister as housekeeper. Len Simmonds's revolutionary gesture ended with his daughter first teaching in the next county, visiting in a smart roadster on weekends, and finally marrying a young dentist. Now the pattern became clear — there was Len, his daughter well provided for, his own position raised a notch on the social scale (hobnobbing with doctors and dentists), and getting his teeth filled for nothing into the bargain. It was through such pioneering efforts that the way was paved for Sophie's future.

It seemed that she was destined to be a teacher ("good job for a woman," "you can always fall back on teaching," "you can even go back to it after you have children, if the worst comes to the worst"), and her contemplation of the teachers at the Bolton School had taught her that the university-trained teachers had it all over the others. They wore gowns and on Founder's Day embellished them with satin-lined hoods in their university colors. The others had to make do with their best dresses and bits of costume jewelry stuck here and there. But it wasn't just the regalia. There was an understanding in the school that the training college staff, teaching fringe subjects like domestic science, gym, games, and scripture, were less

worthy of consideration. If they had discipline problems, they, and
not the students, were deemed at fault, scorned, and left to manage
as best they could. They moved under a cloud of humiliation, and
Sophie had no wish to be one of them.

All the same, discussions of the subject bothered her. She liked to
work alone, and she seemed to manage all her subjects well enough
so that neither she nor her parents were called in for consultations.
But when she was with her fellow competitors, she was assailed by
doubts. It seemed impossible that she should ever do as well as they.
They had so many advantages, brothers and sisters and even parents
who had been to the grammar school and some to the university.
They had much wider experiences, having visited the universities and
traveled abroad, so that in conversation she felt disadvantaged and
ill-equipped. If she were left alone, blinkered, she could pretend they
did not exist and just work along in her own way. But once she
weighed herself against the others, she became intimidated and
suffered from a failure of nerve.

For this reason, her Grandmother Watson's house was a refuge
where nothing shook her confidence and nothing was demanded of
her. Even conversation was limited and became more so when her
grandmother acquired a television set. These were the early days of
TV and programs were sparse during the day—a children's program
in the morning, a woman's hour in the afternoon, news here and
there. Her grandmother kept the set turned on all day long and listened for when the programs were heralded by a medley of tunes—
"Early One Morning," "Danny Boy," and "The Ash Grove." Then
she would leave her calculations and say "I've got to watch the telly"
with a strong imperative, like someone forced to keep an eye on a
child who couldn't be left alone for a second without inviting disaster. She stationed herself in front of the set, sitting much too close
and staring hard at a puppeteer with immaculately coiffed hair and
enameled face talking to Muffin the Mule or Louise Mouse. Sophie
would have given anything to know the old woman's thoughts, but
she was totally wrapt and inscrutable. She rarely answered questions
anyway. If Sophie asked her something, she often repeated the word
and followed its train of associations into some kind of inner mental
labyrinth.

"Who caught that stuffed trout in the glass case, Granny?"

"Trout? When your grandfather came courting me, he used to wear spats. Spats! You never see them any more!"

"What *are* spats, Granny?"

"And a little moustache. My mother told me, 'I wouldn't put no dependence on a man that thinks so much of hisself.' She never did cotton on to your grandfather."

Only sometimes, before a big race, the excitement in the house was almost palpable, and the grandmother became garrulous. Suddenly she was like someone in the grip of a vision, gifted with total recall of all the races she had ever seen or heard of. She recited their names — Thursby Selling Plate, the Lancashire Hurdle, the Manchester Races, the Liverpool Races, the Earl of Sefton's Stakes. She remembered the jockeys and the owners, the racing colors and the wonderful names of the horses — L'Escargot, Clever Scot, Rag Trade, Curlicue, Golden Miller. She told of going on Jump Sunday to Aintree and inspecting the race course just before the Grand National. She could still name and describe all the jumps — The Chair, Valentine's Brook, The Canal Twin Fence, The Water Jump, and the most dreaded one of all, Beecher's Brook. She told thrilling stories of triumphs and disasters. She told of the loose horse, the one that shed his jockey early and rode the field unguided and uncontrolled, shying at certain jumps, running athwart them, and creating havoc among the oncoming horses and riders; or of loose horses, pounding on and on, taking jump after jump, and completing the course riderless and brave. Sophie at such times was enthralled and inspired.

All the same, these occasions were becoming fewer and fewer all the time. The fact was that, although the old woman said she felt like a two-year-old, her strength and will were weakening. To Sophie this showed itself in the intensification of certain disagreeable traits and in the emergence of new ones. Reading the obituary columns, she noted the deaths with such glee and derision that even Sophie's minimal sense of decorum was offended.

"Well, well, Mrs. Flitcroft popped off at long last."

"So Fred Cleworth's pushin' up daisies I see."

And she questioned Sophie in a malicious way about her other grandmother.

"What does your Granny Lewty do all day long?"

"Why, she reads and rests a lot in bed."

"Well, soon she'll be resting *all the time*. Ha Ha Ha."

"Who does your Granny Lewty's work?"

"Me, Mum, and Mrs. Hodkinson."

"Aye, she never was one for liftin' a finger to help herself."

Sophie was protective of her soft, pudgy grandmother, and these comments deeply annoyed her. She told her mother, "Me Granny Watson's downright cheeky a lot of the time." Her mother smiled and said, "Oh, you've found that out at long last, have you?" In her exchanges with Sophie's mother, the grandmother was even more cantankerous.

"I see where Ronnie Brand went. He didn't leave much neither. Must have spent it all on show."

"On the other hand," said Sophie's mother, "perhaps he enjoyed himself, while he could."

"I see Mrs. Harriet Johnson's gone. And hardly left enough for a decent funeral. Wonder what she did with it all."

"Perhaps she gave some away before she went. Some have more sense than to let it all go in death duties."

"Makes no difference what it goes on where she is."

"It doesn't," said Sophie's mother, "but I wouldn't want to slave every day of my life in a butcher's shop to give it all to the government while my son and his wife live in a pokey little cottage down the jig. And *I've* just about given up trying to get this grate clean, that's another mug's game," and she slammed out of the house, leaving Sophie open-mouthed from shock, and her grandmother tee-heeing softly over her racing form.

One spring Sophie went on a school trip to the Lake District for several days. Returning home, she met her father leaving the house, and said to him, "Why are you wearing that arm band?" He took her hand, leading her back to the house, and told her that while she was on holiday, her Grandmother Watson had died and been buried. Her grandmother for the past year had been impossibly obstinate and unpleasant ("mangy," Sophie's mother called her, and "nowt"), and Sophie could hardly believe how little she minded the loss. It was several days before her parents could bring themselves to announce the crucial fact about her grandmother's death. Sophie was doing the crossword in the paper one evening when her mother said, "You might as well tell her."

"Sophie," her father said, "your Granny Watson left you all her money."

"She did?" said Sophie. "What did she do that for?"

"To spite me," said her mother.

"Now Betsy," said her father, "we don't know what she had in mind. It could have been worse."

"Oh yes," said her mother. "It could have all gone to the injured jockeys or to our Fan. It makes me proper blazing. And after we called her after your Aunt Sophie that never left her a penny."

"Is it very much?" asked Sophie.

"As a matter of fact, yes, it's a very great deal," said her father. "She had a lot more than anybody thought."

"Well, where did she get it?" asked Sophie, thinking of the stuffy house, the moth-eaten fur coat, and the stews that always tasted the same.

"I bet she came up on the football pools and never let on," said her mother.

"Nonsense, Bet," said her father. "You heard what the solicitor said as well as I did. She was a very wise woman in financial matters and made some very shrewd investments."

"When can I have it?" said Sophie.

"Well now," said her father, "we shall have to look into that." Looking into it took the form of a discussion with her teachers, and for this purpose the whole family journeyed together to the school. The trip was made easier by a neighbor who offered to take them along in his car when he went to do some shopping at Bolton market.

Sophie's parents had occasionally visited the school to attend open houses, plays, and parents' evenings, but they had never met the new headmistress who had been in office for the past two years. She received them in her study, and Sophie could tell that her parents didn't know what to make of her. She wasn't your usual headmistress with scraped-back hair and a gaunt face. She was young and well dressed, with wild, curly hair, and, most unusual of all, she was a "Mrs."

Sophie's father said, "We were wondering about the chances of our Sophie going to the university."

"And why ever not?" said the headmistress. "She has been in the university stream throughout. Is it a question of financial difficulty?"

"No, it isn't," said her mother with pride. "That wasn't what we were wondering about."

"I can assure you," said the headmistress, "that Sophie is quite capable of handling university work and coming out with flying colors. Her records show that she has an excellent mathematical mind."

"A mathematical mind!" cried her mother in a very shocked voice. "Well I don't know where she got *that!*"

"What would a woman do with a mathematical mind?" asked her father in a more reasonable tone of voice. Sophie wanted to sink right through the floor, but the headmistress gave her a broad smile and a wink. She said, "Well, there are very many jobs these days in a wide range of areas. Industry, for example."

"Industry!" cried her mother in a shrill voice, as if she had just spotted a cockroach on the rug.

For weeks afterwards this visit was the sole subject of conversation in the household. Sophie's future and her newly revealed talents were endlessly discussed, and Sophie moved about the house under a cloud of illegitimacy. When interest in that topic flagged slightly, they took up the phenomenon of the headmistress.

"I wonder what her husband does."

Some of the questions Sophie was able to answer.

"He's the classics master at the Boys' Grammar School." (Her father snorted with laughter at this and said, "I wonder which one's the boss when they're at home.")

Her mother said, "Did you see her wink at our Sophie? You wouldn't think a woman in her position" . . . and so it went on around and around, the same comments coming up day after day. Often Sophie tuned out and thought her own thoughts, humming tunes under her breath, tuning in to the conversation and out again: "winking . . . not very ladylike" . . . "fancy her husband letting her"

. . . "Sophie says she drives her own car" . . . "well she must make a penny in her position" . . . "imagine winking at our Sophie" . . . .

Sophie, all this while, sat in her own world dreaming of her future. She felt like a person who has been sitting for a long time in a darkened room and, when someone bustles in suddenly and flings open the curtains, is amazed to see the sun shining outside. Her mother said, "When you go away to this 'ere university, our Sophie, you won't find home cooking. Oh no, you won't."

"I expect I shall survive," said Sophie.

"You know how you always want seconds of pudding. You with your sweet tooth."

"Hum, yes," said Sophie.

"*Which* you get from your Grandfather Lewty."

"Perhaps," said Sophie, "perhaps."

A Spectator Sport

English grammar schools, like English towns, are often comfortably haphazard as if, instead of being planned, they grew by some natural process and assimilated various architectural styles along the way. Thus, a converted vicarage might be tacked on to a Nissen hut, and both of them attached by a clumsy walkway to a new concrete building housing some modern facility like a science lab or a gymnasium.

The Bromleigh School was entirely different in this respect. It had been liberally endowed by a rich manufacturer of soaps and detergents. No effort had been spared in its design and no expense in its execution. The exterior was of fine red sandstone and the interior — from the vaulted ceiling of the great hall down to the parquet floors and the individual students' desks — was of solid oak.

If there was any incongruity about the place, it was a certain schizophrenia in the image that the school presented by suggesting at the same time a military fortress and a convent. The martial aspect of the central arch was denied by the motto emblazoned above it: BLESSED BE THE PEACEMAKERS. The crenelated towers and battlements were contradicted by the interior cloisters, which suggested silent meditation.

On our side of the central arch — the Girls' Division — the atmosphere was predominantly monastic. We were required to change into soft-soled shoes before we trod the parquet floors. Running was forbidden, hurrying frowned upon, and shouting a punishable offense. The corridors were pervaded by a Sabbath hush and the smell of floor polish; the entire school was kept, true to the conception of the first Lord Bromleigh, immaculate.

I have no means of knowing what it was like on the other side, for that mysterious region, at once so near and so remote, housed the Boys' Division. It might be expected that an enterprising or curious student could have stepped across from one side to the other. Physically, it would have been easy, but no one ever did that. The taboo was too strong, the fear of retribution too great. The two schools remained as isolate and separate as if the entire town of Bromleigh stood between them.

As a matter of fact, the astonishing thing was that the whole town of Bromleigh did *not* stand between them. Girls' and Boys' branches of grammar schools in all the surrounding towns were by time-honored custom thus separated. I am not sure whose mad heterosexual fantasy had resulted in the strange yoking of our schools. Did the first Lord Bromleigh pause in his purveying of cleaning fluids long enough to entertain unclean thoughts? Did notions of something beyond sterility float among his sudsy dreams? Perhaps the family tradition of naming thoroughbred racing fillies for the Girls' Division was not an innocent ploy that produced jokes on the platform on Founder's Day, but the indication of a sinister bent. Maybe the illustrious Founder envisaged the two sexes benefiting from common endeavors, profiting from innocent intercourse in sports and the arts.

And, indeed, oral tradition did recall a golden age of joint plays, debates, and renderings of the Hallelujah chorus. Unfortunately, these prelapsarian collusions resulted in more cooperation than was seemly. There were forbidden couplings under the benches of the biology lab and even, it was rumored, an unwanted offspring, presumably not named, like Lord Bromleigh's fillies, for the Girls' Division. Whatever the truth of this lore, the schools in my day conducted their choral concerts and plays independently. We did our Shakespearean plays in reverse Elizabethan manner with the girls taking all the parts. The boys did theirs, more authentically and much more successfully, with an all-male cast.

Such practices were entirely in keeping with the philosophy of our

school, which was to erase as far as possible all consciousness of
gender. Our school uniform was carefully designed with this intent.
Its chief item was a gym tunic, straight up and down with great box
pleats fore and aft. This garment was a great leveler for it made us
all look like well-upholstered oil drums. Underneath, we wore navy-
blue knickers so long in the legs that when the elastic snapped, they
dropped far below the hem of the tunic. We also wore men's shirts,
ties, and flat-laced outdoor shoes. If we were reduced to the status of
objects, they were definitely not sex objects.

It is, however, a fact universally acknowledged that repression
does not necessarily produce asceticism. Did not the abstinence of
the mystics help to foster wonderful visions? So with us. The dis-
couragement of normal sexual awareness did not so much increase
our studiousness as awaken myriad dreams and fantasies. Curious
alignments, strange reveries with curlicues and exotic embroideries
unfolded in our minds, convoluted and delicate and rare as the in-
sides of seashells. Let no one grow clinical and use latinate words like
sublimation, aberration, and *autoeroticism,* for we knew none.
They were the language of an unknown country to which we had
neither map nor access. Incest we confused with setting fire to hay-
stacks, orgasm with rudimentary forms of animal life like jellyfish,
and copulation seemed most likely to be carried on by foreigners
across the channel. Sex was the undiscovered country from whose
bourne no traveler returned, at least not to talk to us about it. It was
a great uncharted continent and the distance to it from where we
were was as far and impossible and alluring as the distance to the farthest star. It was our brave new world, our America, our perhaps-
never-to-be-found-land.

Nevertheless, the inchoate impulses that made the first Lord
Bromleigh create schools so extraordinarily conjoined were perhaps
approved by a higher power, for they did at last achieve fulfillment.
In spite of all the precautions of the headmistress and her staff and
the headmaster and his staff, the two student bodies were—if not
flung into each other's arms — at least brought into much closer prox-
imity than those in authority could have imagined or condoned.

If peace was our scourge, war proved to be our salvation, for it
prevented the completion of the grand design for the school. All the

workmen and materials were channeled into the war effort before the school was quite finished. Consequently, the Girls' Division lacked a swimming pool and the Boys' Division, oh joy, lacked a dining room. It was easy for us to forego aquatic skills, and the boys were rarely disturbed at their studies by hearing us singing each to each in their pool. But the dining room was an entirely different matter, for they had to eat. In order to do so, all 555 boys made a daily route march from their school to ours, along our cloister and into the dining room. Strict rules were enforced, naturally. The dining room itself was declared out of bounds. So were the corridors all around the dining room. The cloister leading to the dining room was sealed off. The first floor bathrooms were closed. The garden outside the dining room windows was forbidden. In short, it was impossible for any girl to meet A Boy face to face. But, since we had dined early in order to free our facilities for the boys, it was impossible to herd us back immediately into the classrooms, and we were still at large when the boys made their trek. Thus developed the great school sport of Watching the Boys, beside which lacrosse, netball, rounders, tennis, and cricket were as nothing.

Each day when the hour struck, out we came from every corner of the schools — girls of all shapes and sizes, little ones and big ones, fat ones and thin ones, hale ones and lame ones. In summer we stretched out on the turf. In winter we stood mute and frozen, but to a girl we indulged in the same gloating voyeurism. The younger ones were undiscriminating, idly curious, less famished in their attention. The older ones were already developing connoisseurs' eyes for shapely limbs, well-rounded thighs, airy brows. And always, here and there, someone incubated a passion for her Chosen One so overwhelming that it became legendary throughout the school. To such a girl, her own forced absences from school were catastrophic; the absences of the Chosen One, days of torment; and school holidays periods of acute suffering, dreaded, endured, and only barely survived.

Thus our introduction to The Opposite Sex. Was this what the headmistress had in mind when, in her initial interview with each incoming student and her parents, she asked her ritual question: "Does she understand the facts of life?" Many parents, as they contemplated the curious personage of Miss Dorothea Marley, must have asked themselves if she did. She was a woman of breathtaking ugliness, rivaling the Duchess in *Alice in Wonderland,* a combination of something from a different time or a different world. Of indeterminate sex, she wore an Eton crop hairdo, thick stockings, and flesh-mortifying tweed suits. Her antique shoes had spool heels and bars across the front. No one knew where she found them because they were no longer available in any shops. It was her boast, carried over from her days as a young headmistress, that she knew the name of every girl in the school. By our day she had reached a premature senility and could not remember any names at all, neither those of girls nor of staff members, and it was said that she sometimes had to look up her own name in the Bromleigh telephone directory.

Because my friend and I shared the same name, however, she remembered it and pounced on us whenever she saw us, eager to prove her once-good memory.

"And where is The Other Janet today?"

"And where is your Fidus Achates today?"

I regret growing up before the phrase "role model" gained currency because we might have spent some entertaining hours speculating on the origin of this strange being, who when she retired received many accolades — "guided the school through many important years of change and growth . . ." "ever mindful as she piloted the school as a whole, of the needs of the most insignificant of its members. . . ."

She seemed to us to be more mindful of the needs of horses who were being shipped from Ireland in "the most inhumane of conditions" to be slaughtered for consumption in France. I don't know why she deemed it her special responsibility to intervene in this satisfactory and remunerative arrangement between the two countries, but she did. All our fund-raising efforts were directed toward this cause, and whenever the *Bromleigh Evening News* asked the heads of schools to write editorials, instead of writing on the anticipated subjects relating to education, careers for women, or some such, she wrote about horses. I remember once at a small tea given in her study for a visiting lecturer to which forced attendance was meted out on a rotating basis, she said that perhaps the level that any society had reached could be judged by its treatment of animals. She spoke with very great precision and pronounced society "societah." When she had uttered, she smiled her beatific smile and looked around as if she had voiced words of infinite wisdom. We all thought she was dotty.

"A happy school." This was part of the legend. Miss Marley used the phrase when she retired, and her successor responded that it was easy to be happy in a place of so much beauty. I think she referred to the oak bannisters, the red sandstone, and the parquet floors.

Most of us survived the pressures of the place because, as adolescents, we were buoyant, hopeful, confident in the future, and adept at contriving amusements and compensations.

I had fallen in love with language and literature and found a real, substantial joy in reading Shakespeare. The Other Janet was also immersed in literature but more jauntily somehow, for she was less dreamily romantic than I. She had acquired—perhaps from the secondhand book stall at Bromleigh market—an ancient edition of John Donne's works. It was old enough to have the archaic script and small enough to slip in the pocket of her gym tunic. She carried it always on her person as her one indispensable text, her Bible, her weapon, her talisman. Every memory of these years is punctuated with fragments of a Fong or Fonnet by John Donne. Usually these were lines about fex, or fummer, or the fun, but the ancient calligraphy had so influenced her own speech that it was hard to say where Donne ended and she began.

If our present pleasures were in literature, language, laughter, there was always the promise of something more exciting at the end of the prison corridor of school, along which we crept in our soft-soled shoes for seven years, hardly daring to breathe or sneeze. The be-all and end-all of our discipline and deprivation and study was the celestial city of Oxbridge, waiting with its gleaming spires and waterways and all its beauty and excitement and loveliness. When we spoke its name, we saw our future selves rushing down the High, our undergraduate gowns floating on the breeze. Usually we were surrounded by a bevy of male students (the ratio of men to women was notoriously favorable there) who were boatered, blazered, gowned, old-school tied, titled, and distinguished. In other manifestations, we saw ourselves punting on the river, sipping champagne and nibbling strawberries at May balls, or merely walking through the meadows on quiet Sunday afternoons. Studying? Reading? I don't remember that we thought too much about that. It was mostly the gowns and parties and suitors, our vision of the Emerald City. Some day, some day.

If that was our distant future, there was something nearer which combined present diversions with prospects of future enjoyment — the summer holidays, which for us meant *Abroad*. Through the school, it was arranged that most of us could spend a month or two with a French or German family. The motives for such an excursion in my case were fairly complicated. My mother had the idea that I would improve my French accent and, along with it, my chances of getting into a good university. French was a required subject and my mother was a practical woman. The school's attitude was more sophisticated. The staff felt they provided quite enough in the way of teaching the language — grammar, pronunciation, and even accent. But they knew there was more to learning the language. They wanted us to live with a French family in order to understand The French Way of Life. For us, the students, the journey needed no justification. Apart from the fact that we were madly francophilic, the journey offered our first excursion into The Outside World beyond the confines of our own homes and families. Suddenly, it seemed that the World at Large, the Continent, Abroad, even Life itself was being opened to us like a great three-dimensional movie on a wide screen.

I had an additional reason for the journey to France, for I had a grandmother. As a matter of fact, I had two living grandmothers, and they can hardly have been more different. One was extremely worldly, and it seems now a great paradox that she remains the more shadowy of the two. She returns to me only in fragments — disembodied fingers, pudgy and beringed, dipping into boxes of chocolates; a big untidy bed with a pink bedspread and lots of newspapers, books, and magazines; a cluttered dressing table with scent and powder and hair. She seemed not at all old and, when she was not in bed resting, she went about a great deal to play bridge and meet friends. Altogether, she was a very jolly, card-playing, loud-laughing, martini-loving, present-bearing, cigarette-smoking, flowery-hat-wearing, roly-poly grandmother.

The other grandmother was patently not of this world and this time. She was old, shriveled, unfathomable, and burdened by griefs too various and inarticulate to count — daughters lost to dubious religions, sons killed in the war, property dispersed, hopes shattered, grandchildren alienated, friends dead and gone. She lived in a world half of the living and half of the dead, and her house was a museum of cracked paintings, yellowing photographs, stuffed fish in glass cases, heavy curtains, dark wood, gloomy alcoves, ugly Victoriana, stuffy heat.

It occurs to me for the first time that my grandmothers' early lives must have been very similar. Their losses were the same — daughters to unsuitable husbands, sons to the war, husbands to untimely deaths. Both were widows and lived alone in their oversized family homes — but what made one a merry widow and the other a guardian of the dead?

When I visited my jolly grandmother, which I did every week, she gave me things, bestowing them in a kind of ceremony. Upstairs in her bedroom she handed over a glass necklace, a brooch, always chocolates individually wrapped in shiny paper, peppermints, treacle toffee, and forbidden drinks — sherry, cherry brandy, colored cordials — with the cautionary phrase, "Don't let on to your Ma about this." She disliked my mother, and maybe that's why she gave me the drinks I was not allowed to have. She slipped a half a crown into my coat pocket when I left. We laughed a great deal, and yet I can't remember her at all. I feel keenly my disloyalty and ingratitude in that matter.

With my other grandmother, in spite of her impassive face, it seems that I understood her mind and its inner workings. I was her lieutenant taking her on her weekly errand to the cemetery, carrying things, helping. We weeded a bit, pulled up grass that got among the plants, left flowers in the pot. That done, we walked on the path looking critically at the other graves, reading the War Memorial:

THEY SHALL NOT GROW OLD AS WE THAT ARE LEFT GROW OLD.

And then back home to put on the kettle and have some tea and digestive biscuits. There were drinks and chocolates in a cupboard, but they were not offered, being reserved for emergencies. Brandy was for upset stomachs, chocolates for visiting children who had accidents. They all did, for this was a very accident-prone house. The stairs were steep, the floors splintery, the tables too crowded with fragile bric-a-brac. Her conversation was unjolly, and its characteristic was not so much its extreme morbidity as the sense that words spoken were part of a subterranean dialogue that had been blown up, accidentally detonated so that fragments floated to the surface: a reference to my mother's bad heads, to someone who had died. Perhaps it was just in this that I felt akin to her, since I easily slipped into the submarine world of secret reverie.

She sometimes mentioned Alfred, her baby who had been killed along with thousands of Allied soldiers in Normandy. After the war she had been told that he was buried where he had fallen in a certain place. Through the War Office she was able to arrange for the spot to be marked, and there it was, a very little narrow grave in a foreign field. A framed picture on her mantlepiece proved its existence, and none of us realized that she minded not seeing it until the question of my going to France came up. Suddenly the excursion became a package deal, a group tour for the two of us. It was decided that we should go together. Her silent presence could protect me from abductors, child molesters, rapists. In return, I could interpret for her. And, conveniently, she paid all our expenses.

And so, summer after summer, we set off to stay with the family we had selected from the roster of ones available and approved for Bromleigh School girls. Our family was a fortuitous choice. The parents were schoolteachers, and there was a girl, Anne Marie, exactly my own age.

But the great advantage of staying with the Desgranges was that they lived in Gentilly, a suburb of Paris about three metro stops out of the city on the ligne de Sceaux. Their house was small but had a large garden, and we managed very well for the six weeks of our visit. Grandmother and I shared a small bedroom, and she never went into the city at all, but spent her time sitting outdoors under a shady tree. The garden was wildly disordered and un-English, with fallen fruit from the trees lying about rotting and fermenting and attracting wasps, the flowers overgrown and unweeded and rampaging over the paths, lush and straggling everywhere with great tendrils and feelers. Grandmother appeared not to notice the chaos. I think she expected things to be different abroad and put every strange sight down to that one face. She sat totally rapt in her own thoughts. I understood that this was her time for communing with Alfred, so long neglected on her Sunday cemetery visits. I was sure she spent the days going over his life very slowly and repeatedly, as if it were an erotic fantasy growing clearer or dimmer with each repetition until it worked itself out into nothingness. How did I know this? Did she say something? Speak of him? I rather think she never mentioned him at all.

My pleasures were entirely of the present, and at first the simplest things excited me – all the smells and sounds of the little town. I loved going with Anne Marie to the market and bringing home cheeses, fruits, and breads, of kinds previously unknown to me and entirely delicious.

All of us who went to France for the summer were greedy for new sensations, ready to try everything with complete abandon. But there was something compulsive in our enthusiasm for the *boucher chevalier*. It was an act of defiance against Miss Marley, and we ate the meat with a kind of anarchic freedom, regarding the experience as a magic sort of communion, eating, in an annual ritual of cleansing (or the reverse) the very horses we had spent the year trying to save. It was not the horsemeat we ate but the sweet ashes of revenge. I don't know how my grandmother would have reacted to the knowledge that most of the meat she was eating was, at my special request, horsemeat, because I translated it merely as "meat." As official translator I allowed myself considerable leeway, and this practice worked out very happily and smoothed over many areas of potential embarrassment.

Grandmother's meetings with the family were limited to mealtime and enhanced by my adept translations. Before each meal I was sent to the garden with a small aperitif on a tray. This was much appreciated, and I think Grandmother believed that "aperitif" was the name of a region like Bordeaux or Burgundy.

"Tell 'em I like that aperitif."

I relayed the message.

"*Ma grandmère aime bien l'aperitif. Elle veut encore.*" I myself

refused the obviously alcoholic drinks, but I drank huge amounts of
Vouvray, believing it to be a kind of French lemonade. I see now that
it is entirely possible Grandmother and I were a little drunk most of
the time, but if I felt dizzy I put it down to the sun. It may have been a
little of both, for I overexposed myself recklessly to the sun. The
Desgranges family observed me with rapture.

"*Elle boit le soleil, la p'tite Anglaise.*"

They were proud of their sun. They loved to see us overindulge
and overeat and encouraged our shameless greed with cries of "*profitez-en!*" "*Profitez-en!*" I think they suspected that our normal life
in England was a steady mortification of the palate, and perhaps
they were right.

Fortified by quantities of aperitif, my grandmother enjoyed her
food. Her table manners were not delicate, since she no longer had
her own teeth. She pulled and gnawed at bread and meat in a way
that caused my mother some alarm, and real anguish if they had to
eat together in public places. There was oilcloth instead of a table-
cloth at the Desgranges, and when in our haste and hilarity we spilled
a great deal of wine and water, we laughed and called ourselves "*la
famille de la flaque d'eau à table.*"

I quickly learned to break off a lump of bread and mop up every
scrap of delicious juice on my plate, and so did Grandmother.

"I like this gravy," she said, and I translated, "*Ma grandmère
adore la sauce. Elle trouve que c'est extrêmement delicieux. Delicieuse.*"

Immediately more would be poured onto her plate with elaborate
gestures of goodwill and cries of "*profitez-en.*" "No" was not taken
for an answer. The horsemeat was very tender for my grandmother
to chew, and she asked to find out how they got it so soft. I was told,
"*On le met dans une marinade de l'ail et de vin et de champignons
pendant douze heures et puis. . . .*"

"They soak it in wine. . . ."

"Oh. Well, whatever they do, it's good. How do they get these
chips so good?"

"They have olive oil in the chip pan, Granny."

"Oh."

"*Ma grandmère trouve que la cuisine française est extrêmement delicieux. Delicieuse.*"

At the end of the meal, *digestifs* were produced and much enjoyed by my grandmother. Then she went to bed for a siesta after lunch and an early night after supper. Normally a fitful sleeper, she was sleeping soundly for long hours and thought that the climate suited her.

Anne Marie and I, when our digestive systems had recovered from the onslaught of the last meal, went into the city. The Desgranges were very kind and constantly organized excursions. On Sundays we went on all-day outings to Fontainebleau and Versailles, and on weekdays we went into Paris to see Montmartre, Notre Dame, the Eiffel tower, and the Louvre. But what I loved most were the times we sat in the late afternoon sun in some café along the Champs Elysées, sipping Vouvray, chilled and bubbly, and watching the people go by. It seemed that in this parade of cheerful, colorful holiday-makers I saw a panorama of my whole future life. There must have been passersby on the boulevards who were not bright and young and carefree. After all, Paris is full of seamstresses, office workers, vagabonds, old people. I saw none of them. My eyes were only for young men in lederhosen; beautiful American women, expensively dressed and enameled; ugly American men with cropped heads like convicts or pin-feathered chickens, but patently rich and self-assured. I watched the lovers at the surrounding tables, their arms loosely entwined. The rapt attention which they trained on each other was nothing to the fixity of the gaze I turned on them.

"Oh la la!" said Anne Marie, "how you make big eyes at people! *Que tu écarquilles des yeux!*"

What a variety of possibilities of light and love and laughter were spread before me on those hot afternoons. I never wanted to stop looking. What were Notre Dame, the Eiffel Tower, or the Louvre to this?

And thus the summer passed swiftly. Fummer's leafe had all too fhort a date for me. Soon it was the end of August, and Anne Marie was seeing us off at the Gare du Nord, screaming as the train pulled out, "*Au revoir, Jeanne. A l'année prochaine! Bon courage pour la rentrée! Bon courage! Courage. . . . Courage!*"

But the journey was not over. For my grandmother the most important part came next. Or perhaps it was not the most important part. Possibly she had relived all her life with Alfred in that shady part of the Desgranges garden, reaching a kind of exultation with the aperitifs and the *digestifs* so that the visit to the grave itself was simply a formality, a leave-taking. I always puzzled about how it happened that we found the grave as we did. The farmer and his wife escorted us formally out there, and it was always the same — quite well kept up but with weeds. I think that before we arrived they stopped weeding it so that my grandmother could have the satisfaction of pulling up some weeds and setting the grave to rights. She tidied it up and, having performed that ritual, left it for another year.

I was much fatter and very sunburned and my mother looked at me with satisfaction and said, "The change has done you good." My jolly grandmother was jealous and said, "If I had your Granny Parker's money, we'd go around the world. First class all the way."

Somehow that didn't tempt me. Paris was the utmost I yearned for. Already I was anxious about next year, for I never knew from one year to the next whether our excursion would be off or on.

My grandmother was not to be pressed on the subject, and every Sunday I patiently accompanied her to the cemetery, carrying trowels, Michaelmas daisies, and chrysanthemums, waiting for her mind to drift at last to the grave across the sea. Finally, during the daffodil season, it happened: "We'll take 'em some bulbs, in t' summer."

On Monday I couldn't wait to see The Other Janet.

"Fair stands the wind for France, Janet."

"Oh, fuper, Janet."

And so another year turned, and the summer came round again, and we set off on our journey. My earlier sense of excitement had been replaced by something more satisfying. I was developing intellectual and aesthetic interests. I read a great deal of French history and French literature. The boulevards didn't lose their fascination for me, but I was now enthralled in a different way by Fontainebleau and Versailles. The paintings in the Louvre absorbed me, and I stood in front of them for long hours in an ecstasy of concentration. Anne

Marie beside me was frantic with impatience, "Always you stare and stare. *Tu veux boire les peintures? Oh alors, allons! Que j'ai soif. . . .*"

"*Encore un moment,* Anne Marie, and we'll be off, but *encore un moment. . . .*"

I carried a notebook and wrote down all that I wished to remember. I wanted my impressions to remain as permanent as the epitaphs carved in marble on gravestones. Today when I look at my jottings they read like haiku:

Le hameau de Marie Antoinette,
    Our picnic in the woods at Fontainebleau

Anne Marie sitting on a nest of fourmi
    My éclat de rire infuriates her

Jeanne, you never stop choking,
    Always you choke. Oh la la!

La joconde not shown to advantage,
    Glass frame, bad light, small in scale

A lovers' quarrel in the café on the Boul Mich
    Andromache at the Comedie Française

Café au lait and croissants
    Bright sun. A painting by Matisse

Anne Marie tells me "Tu est grosse,
    mais tu la portes avec beaucoup de grace." I'm livid.

Everyone tired and out of spirits,
    The fruit rotten-ripe in the garden

The setting sun reminds Anne Marie
    Of a fromage Hollandaise. She lacks ésprit

The fountains of Versailles,
    The cobblestones of Fontainebleau

Spectacle de son et de lumière
    at the Chateau de Sceaux

Ginkgo trees at the Cité Université
    feu d'artifice beyond the horizon.

Anne Marie would never concede that my studies were as demanding as hers. It was a point of national honor for her to stress how
much more difficult her examinations were, how remote the chance
of her passing them. "Certainly, I shall not be received," she said,
when she spoke of them. She made great sweeping gestures with her
arms to illustrate the height of the *niveau* and vast number of
students who were not going to be received. Perhaps she was right,
but I could not imagine anyone working harder than I was doing for
the exams at the end of my final year. I had so much Latin and
French and English and, if I failed, I should not be able to go to the
university. Even if I didn't fail, I might not do well enough to win one
of the open scholarships. In that event, Oxbridge would be out of the
question, and I would have to go instead to one of the obscure redbrick universities in the provinces. I worked so hard that I had trouble sleeping and had a sick feeling always in my stomach. My mother
watched me anxiously because some girls got "brain-fag" and had to
give up.

I could think of very little besides the exams, and when one Sunday my grandmother said, "We'll take one of them urns next summer," I was pleased, but the summer seemed very far away. I tried in
odd moments to lose myself in daydreams. I was suddenly uninter-
ested in the Boys' Division and could not work up any enthusiasm for
my Chosen One of the year. The population of desirable boys seemed
to have diminished or passed on to Oxbridge.

I thought hopefully of France. I had read a book about two Oxford women who went to Versailles and met numbers of people
dressed in old-fashioned, unfamiliar clothes. Later, when they described their meetings to other people, they discovered that they had
seen the gardeners and courtiers and characters of an earlier time.
All their descriptions were checked and corroborated and proved
correct. The women were highly reputable scholars. I didn't believe
the account. It sounded too much like the kind of thing Janet and I
would dream up, but I was still fascinated by it. I dreamed of going
to Versailles and being mentally transported to a different age. When
I read my French history books, I dreamed of meeting the people,
and during the long bus rides to school I invented the accounts of
these meetings.

If I could just survive the year of studying and the exams, everything would be fine. After France there would be one more year at school, but it would be a relaxed year doing interviews at the various Oxbridge colleges, buying clothes and books in preparation for my new life ahead.

I did survive the year and the exams, but only barely. I felt no immediate sense of relief when the last exam was finished, and wondered if my uncertainty about the results was weighing on me. My mother was not unduly worried. She said, "You're run down from all the studying. The change abroad will do you good."

Even my grandmother came out of her own thoughts long enough to stare at me and say, "Something's ailing you. What's the matter with you?" The Desgranges noticed the difference and said, "*Elle est souffrante, la p'tite anglaise. Elle est tout à fait énervée.*" They too had confidence in their sun, their food, their France. They brought colored drinks in little glasses the size of eggcups and urged me to drink the full-bodied red wines. I did that, but nothing helped. I could no longer profit from any of it. There was something going wrong with my mind. When I walked to the market, instead of being delighted by the sights and smells, I noticed alarming sights that I had overlooked before. There were bullet holes in many of the buildings in the village and there were signs:

ICI JEAN-LUC LEGROS EST TOMBÉ POUR LA FRANCE,

VICTIME DE L'OCCUPANT ALLEMAND.

ICI, LE 5 SEPTEMBRE 1943, ANTOINE CALAMEL

EST MORT POUR LA PATRIE.

These were memorials to young men who had been dragged out by the Gestapo while their families and friends and the villagers stood watching helplessly. Once in Paris, Anne Marie said to me, "*Voilà la crematorium où les Boches ont tenu les patriotes pour enlever leurs yeux et leurs bras.*"

I did not need to jot these things in my notebook. I needed some way to erase them from my mind. They haunted me so insistently that when someone at the next table laughed suddenly and stridently, I jumped in my seat and wished them dead on the ground.

Even Versailles looked tawdry and fly-blown. The rooms were not peopled by La Pompadour and Du Barry but with the victims of the Ancien Régime. My imagination was crowded with scenes of cruelty and torture—the guillotine, the strappado, the garotte, the bastinado. . . .

The summer was not a success, and when Anne Marie saw me off, she didn't shriek as the train pulled out. She said to me very earnestly, "*Eh bien, ma gosse, ne t'inquiètes pas trop . . .*" and hugged me with feeling, protectively. I cried all the way to Brittany. My grandmother, silent and unamazed, watched me.

She had her own thoughts. The War Graves Commission had asked to move Alfred's remains to one of the big military cemeteries where the white crosses marked an incredible number of anonymous dead. The family wanted her to agree to this transfer because they could use the land in the field now occupied by Alfred's grave. Finally Grandmother had consented, and the body was to be disinterred.

One steamy morning we went out in a silent group to the field, Grandmother and I, the farmer and his wife, and the workmen who were to dig up the grave. We were fortified by café calvas and went in single file across the orchard. But when they dug in the ground, there was nothing there. No coffin, no bones, nothing at all. When Alfred had been blown up, there had been nothing left to bury. If my grandmother was horrified, she showed no sign. We returned to the farm house, drank more café calvas, and then packed our bags and set off immediately for the boat train.

That was our last trip to France together. The following spring my grandmother died and was buried in the cemetery at home. I had suggested that she be cremated in the new crematorium and then scattered in Brittany near where Alfred had died, but my mother poohpoohed the idea. She thought there had been altogether too much of this traipsing off to France on wild-goose chases after nonexistent graves. She had not forgiven France for not sending me back recovered. She kept shaking her head and saying, "I thought the change would do you good," as if the President of the Republic, the government, and the people of France should all be sued for breach of promise. She said, "Grandmother should be buried like everyone else, alongside her husband."

"But Alfred was the one she cared for," I said.

"Stuff," said my mother, "She couldn't abide him."

"What?" I cried.

"Oh, he was quiet and didn't have much go in him. She thought he was lazy and she was always after him. Anyway, that's water under the bridge by now."

I suppose she was right.

I did not, after all, return to the Bromleigh School for the autumn term. I passed all the examinations and won quite a substantial scholarship, but I couldn't face another year in school uniform. I might have done well in the Oxbridge entrance exams, but I decided instead to go to a redbrick university in a fairly big town in the Midlands. My best marks were in French, but English was my first love and I decided to study English literature.

At first I was disappointed with university life. Because of my last-minute arrangements, I was not able to get into a hall of residence or to share a flat with another student. I ended up in digs in a semidetached house at the end of the bus route on the edge of the town. It was all a bit depressing with the slag heaps out the back window, the one bath a week, and the fish-paste sandwiches for high tea.

Nor did I really enjoy my studies. The lecturers were boring and the subjects dull. Really the only difference from school was that we were no longer sexually segregated, but this was not a marked improvement. The English Department consisted overwhelmingly of female students. Of the men, not many were interested in women, and the few who were gravitated to the really attractive women, one of which I definitely was not. It was not at all what I had imaged in those dreams of May balls, strawberries and champagne, punting on the river.

One Sunday I went for a walk to get the taste of the greasy Sunday dinner out of my mouth. It was an overcast day, and I ended up by the canal that ran through that part of town. Leaning over the bridge, I could see myself mirrored in the water, a rippling mirage in a fawn duffel coat. Suddenly a coal barge came under the bridge, manned by a fat barge-woman in a black pinafore and pixy hood. She looked back at me as the barge moved along, and suddenly, in a completely spontaneous gesture, she stuck out her tongue at me as far as it would go. It was a startling act, and I understood that there was nothing personal in it. So I stuck out mine as far as it would go too. Not at her, of course, any more than she had done at me. I was saying, "Yah, old bargee, that's the way I feel, too." I watched her until she was out of sight and then went back to the digs for the fish-paste sandwiches, or maybe it was a Sunday treat like baked beans on toast.

Perhaps my first year at the university, though, was just a period of recovery and adjustment. I worked as a waitress during the summer, and the second year I was admitted to a women's residence hall. Life again assumed a certain dignity. There were formal dinners in the hall, all of us gowned for the occasion; sherry with the matron and warden of the hall before Sunday lunch; visiting faculty members to dinner. . . . I had a pleasant study overlooking the grounds, and beyond that I could see sheep grazing in green fields. It was very charming and bucolic. I enjoyed my fellow students, and also, at this time, I fell in love with my tutor. I suppose this sounds half-baked and adolescent (he had married a student some years earlier and was already raising a second family), but it was not. It gave me a sense of euphoria, and buoyed by this, I regained my passion for literature and life. When I took my finals, I did exceptionally well. Even though I did not have one of the prestigious Oxbridge degrees, I did well enough to find a job in a school as prominent as the Bromleigh School. It was not physically as impressive as the Bromleigh, but I liked the students and staff and enjoyed being on the other side of the educational process. The Other Janet had left Oxbridge before she graduated in order to get married. She was vastly amused at the thought of me as a teacher, and sent me a congratulatory message which said:

> Three cheerf on your Pofition.
> (Render unto Cefar that which is Cefar's).

The Testament of Leyla

The twin cities of Sodom and Gomorrah stood at the farthest end of the great salt lake. They were the most beautiful of the five cities of the plains, and Leyla, the wife of the rich merchant Lot, never stopped marveling at their loveliness. No matter how oppressed she was by the deprivations of her daily life, she was always soothed by the beauty of her surroundings — by the salt flats of Sodom and the green, fertile groves of Gomorrah. It seemed to her a strange thing that in such a setting, which contained everything necessary to human life and happiness, she should have so little of either life or happiness.

Why, she often asked herself, had her life become so deprived? It seemed, looking back, as if it had grown narrower and narrower and narrower, even more narrow, as if she were standing on a piece of land that was being slowly and surely eaten away by the sea. And yet, it could always be worse. That was the one single thought that saved her from self-pity. There were worse instances of human deprivation. In some places people were starving and dying of disease and want and every kind of physical affliction. And yet. . . .

Always she thought back to her early life as a time of the most pure and unspoiled happiness. The place had not been so beautiful, of course. There had been no wide stretch of water and none of the trees she had grown to love on the plains — the great cedars with their gnarled barks and trunks, the olive trees with their delicate green colors and slender leaves whitening in the morning breeze. It had

been rather a dry and arid place, but all the same, it came back to her
mind's eye sparkling with light and sunshine and laughter. She remembered the family compound and the women all together. They
were really doing nothing that was fun — it was odd — and yet she remembered it most happily. The silly thing was that what she
remembered most fondly was washing — yes, washing. She remembered them all together — her sisters and old blind Hannah, working
or sitting around the wash pots, laughing and gossiping and telling
stories. It had all been so simple and untroubled. How had it possibly
happened, she asked herself, that it had ended, that she had let it all
slip away. She had let it be taken from her without the slightest resistance, as though it were the easiest thing in the world to have peace
and happiness, toss it away casually, and catch it again.

Fixing blame, she knew, was unprofitable and unfair. And yet.
. . . And yet she couldn't escape it. She blamed him. Lot. It was all
his fault. Why had he not let her be? Why had he married her in the
first place? And why had her family pushed her into it? It was true
she hadn't resisted. But she didn't know enough to. She was too
young and had no capacity to imagine. Her mind and judgment were
confused by everyone else's response — by the congratulations, by
the talk of honor and good fortune, and by the whole family ex-
claiming about his fine qualities. A rich man, a successful man! A
man of integrity, of virtue. "Any man who honors his mother as Lot
does must make a good husband," her father said in that voice of
masculine authority that brooked no contradiction. The great oracle
had spoken and declared Lot a loyal son and, therefore, a devoted
husband. How those words had rung in her head all that first bitter
summer of their marriage, in the suffocating heat and airless misery.

Lot's celebrated love of his mother was a subject on which she had
meditated constantly. He had lived with her most of his life and had
been inconsolable when she died, and had then married Leyla to fill
the empty space. All that first summer Leyla, in her puzzlement and
confusion, had not known what really ailed her until finally she managed, uninformed and inexperienced as she was, to articulate two
phrases, silently at first and then aloud at last:

HE WANTED A REPLACEMENT FOR HIS MOTHER, TOOK ME, AND NOW FINDS
ME WANTING.

HE HATES ME.

Only old blind Hannah had seen through him. No exclamations
and congratulations came from her. Leyla's sisters pressed her constantly, "Aren't you happy for her Hannah?" "She'll be a married
woman, a mother. There'll be little ones for you to hold."

And Hannah had said, "Marry a man from Sodom?" and laughed
so hard that it was like a death rattle in her old ropy throat. And the
sisters said "old gloompot" and "death's head" behind Hannah's
back. Leyla's mother had looked annoyed, and said sharply to old
Hannah, "You don't want to believe everything you hear. Besides,
look how lovely and young she is. How could anyone help but love
her?"

Looking back, when Leyla thought of her marriage, it seemed to
her like the sacrifice of Isaac by his horrible old father. Oh, she'd
heard that story often enough, and it struck her as thoroughly
obscene. The old man had really been ready to kill his son and had
earned great praise for his steadfastness and piety.

At the time, of course, she had been carried away by all the excitement — being the center of attention in her wedding gown, the wreath
on her head (more appropriate to a funeral), the veil, the armful of
trailing flowers, and all the feasting and laughter and music. How
she had nearly died with pride when Lot gave her the ornate breast-
pin that had belonged to Haran, his mother (the only trinket he ever
gave her), and all her sisters had looked on enviously and oohed and
aahed.

She was absolutely furious with old Hannah, who kept to her
room and refused to meet the bridegroom — "A foreigner was bad
enough," she said, "but a Sodomite! What kind of a family would
marry its daughters to Sodomites?" Leyla's parents were angry too,
and said the old are very difficult and get odd notions and, really,
they should be kept apart from the family. They have such a bad influence on impressionable young girls.

But now, there was a curious thing about old Hannah—this story Leyla had never told anyone. From the time it was arranged that she was to marry Lot, old Hannah had been in a sulk with Leyla, her favorite. She wouldn't speak to her or notice or acknowledge her in the least. And then she grew very ill and kept to her room. Leyla was all taken up with the wedding, looking at gifts, crowing (though pretending not to) over her friends and sisters, and so she neglected the old woman, never went near her at all.

And then, after she went to live in Sodom Heights (all the parts of the city had names which belied the actual terrain), she never thought of Hannah in the least. She never sent messages to her and never even mentioned her in the letters she sent to the rest of the family. But one morning, waking from sleep, she felt a sudden urgency to speak to her, and even before she broke her nightly fast, she sat in her bed-chamber and wrote a letter to Hannah. It was a long, loving letter, as if all the bitterness and resentment between them had fallen away and her clear, lifelong love for Hannah remained untouched.

"Darling Hannah," she wrote, "I do miss you and think of you often." And exaggerating the way one does in letters home, she wrote, "I'm really happy here. It's so beautiful and the climate seems to suit me much better than in the interior. I hardly cough at all any more." And teasing to recall the old times, she said, "I never need the red flannel to wrap up my chest." She could see old Hannah smile at that. And then, really lying, carried away by her own rhetoric and desire to reassure the old folk at home and wanting everyone to be easy in their minds about her, she added at last, "Lot is so kind and considerate. I know you didn't want me to marry him, dear Hannah, but I know I did the right thing."

It was a terrible barefaced lie, and afterwards she thought God might visit a punishment on her for it. (That was how much Lot's way of thinking had begun to permeate her thoughts—this preoccupation with good and bad, right and wrong, punishment and reward, now and in the hereafter.)

Anyway, the lie was canceled because events fell out in such a strange way that all her life Leyla shuddered to think of it. She sent off her letter by special messenger just as soon as possible, but that very day came a letter from her mother telling her that old Hannah had died in the night. Died in the night! Leyla wondered, Had she known that in some mysterious way? Had Hannah spoken to her in her sleep? Had she written the letter before Hannah died, or just after? It was so strange, that sudden urge to speak to her again before it was too late. Sometimes, Leyla thought, our buried urges are strong enough to surge to the surface and make themselves visible.

So Hannah would never know, thought Leyla, that she had had her children after all. She felt guilty about wanting to say "I told you so" to a dead person. And she felt something else too, more discomfiting than guilt. She could hardly admit this to herself, but she knew at last that Hannah was right about Lot. It was by a kind of miracle that she had had children—hardly the product of love and passion. Nor was it that Lot was old. He was, of course, but not all that old, and he kept himself in good shape with regular exercise. He just didn't like women. This she knew intuitively by the way he looked at her disapprovingly in the privacy of their bedroom, insisting that she always be bathing, as if she wasn't capable of judging when she needed to bathe, always afraid she was growing fat.

And his lovemaking, though one could hardly call it that since it was so devoid of love. It was more like a feat, as if he were testing himself by forcing himself to swim just a little farther than he had the strength for. Not at all what she had been lead to believe or had imagined from the strolling players who strummed on their lutes and sang songs of love. Lot needed goblets of wine, though normally he disapproved of drinking wine. And he showed her how to arouse him, though she had understood men were aroused by looking at women and caressing them. The strolling minstrels sang songs about stroking the silky hair and soft breasts of their mistresses. But with Lot it was she who had to stroke and massage, thinking all the while that it was like milking a nasty old billy goat. And when, at last, Lot leaped on top of her, she felt as if she were turned to absolute stone, to a pillar of marble.

But she did, for all that, have children. And Lot was made even more hostile by this. He hated what she knew about him and their bedtime struggles, and in revenge he needed to diminish and humiliate her. So when she produced not sons but first one daughter and

then another, his contempt peaked and his repugnance knew no
bounds, and after that he never touched her again.

And the poor girls, what of them? She felt so sorry for them
because Lot seemed to cloud the very air and the atmosphere of the
house, to make it a desolate place. Even when she entered the door,
there was no denying it, she felt a pall of gloom descend upon her. So
what kind of a life could they have? At least her own childhood
and young womanhood had been sunshiny and cheerful, but they
wouldn't even have that to look back to. Well, which was worse,
after all, being tantalized by memories of a happier time or never
having anything pleasant to remember? It was a toss-up at best.

The only woman Lot approved of was his sister Iscah, a large-
boned woman and the mother of men. Widowed, she refused to
marry again or to allow Lot to manage her affairs. She presided over
her own large house in Gomorrah, traveled when she was inclined to
do so, and generally did exactly as she liked. Although Lot claimed
to believe she was headstrong and in need of masculine guidance, he
had a furtive admiration for her independence and competence, and
his admiration was fanned by family pride. "A woman like my
mother who knows her own mind, a strong character," he said,
thinking perhaps of the subservient and resentful Leyla. Only he
would not have called her Leyla, but Edythe, the name he preferred
and always used.

But if he quietly admired Iscah, he was appalled by her three sons,
who were as feminine as she was masculine and who were frivolous
to boot and filled the house with their boisterous and foolish friends.
Whenever Leyla went there, a party seemed to be in progress with
card games going on and music and feasting. Iscah never made the
slightest effort to conceal anything from Lot. "Come and join the
feast," she would call out in her commanding voice, and Lot would
say that he wished to speak with her alone on a matter of business,
and they would go off and find a quiet courtyard or room and speak
together.

The lads meanwhile would throng about Leyla, making a great
fuss over her, teasing her, complimenting her on her dress and ornaments, stroking her hair, and bringing her treats to eat and drink.
They would tell jokes and make her laugh with their antics and anec-

dotes until she almost got ill. "Leyla, dear, just wait till you find out
what Nahor did the other day when he was drunk. You'll die when
you hear this!" And then they would fall out among themselves
about who should be the one to tell, and all would watch her eagerly
for the first signs of merriment and mirth.

But they weren't by any means as frivolous as they pretended, this
she knew well. For one evening Iscah had prevailed upon her to stay
and spend the evening while Lot was away on a business trip. They
had had a dinner party that night, and the young men had said,
"Let's not drink tonight. Let's have a serious discussion." Nahor
wanted to drink to that, but they all prevented him, telling him that
he had almost drowned in drink the night before and had to mend his
ways. On this particular evening they would not even allow the lute
player to amuse them but sent her on her way. And then they had
talked, such talk and ideas as Leyla had never heard before anywhere. Her head rang for days afterwards.

They talked of love, and each one offered an opinion about it. It
was the first time Leyla had really thought about love, not as something about which the balladeers lied, but as a creative and healing
force, a source of harmony and peace. Iscah brought up the subject
of who had more pleasure in love, men or women; Leyla had never
heard anyone speak on such a subject, let alone speak authoritatively
as Iscah did. Then one of the lads said that he thought the love of
men for women was of a very base kind and not a match for the noble
love of men for men. And Iscah winked boldly at Leyla and said
"What about the love of women for women" so that Leyla blushed to
the roots of her hair. Then finally Nahor put forward a wild theory
about how the sexes had at one time not been separate, but had been
combined in one human form until God split them apart. He said the
two halves subsequently had spent their time trying to merge again
and find their other halves. Then everyone laughed and said Nahor
made no more sense when he was sober than when he was drunk.
And Nahor said, "Well in that case why not pass around the wine."
And so they did that, and the evening passed away pleasantly in
laughter and friendship.

Usually, though, Lot refused to tarry in that house and hurried
away, as if he risked contamination by lingering there. Leyla had

almost to be dragged away and kept looking back longingly to the house, from whence came sounds of laughter and music that carried all the way down the road. "You must visit *us*," she told them hopefully, but they pulled long faces and laughed. Lot's bare hospitality was not to their taste at all.

In fact, the one time they had stopped by had been disastrous. They happened to call one night when Lot was entertaining a group of the serious young men who often visited and whom he addressed as his brethren because they were pious and tried to propagate the word of the Lord. Leyla found them as tedious and disapproving as Lot himself, and even the girls, starved as they were for the company and conversation of young men, had nothing to say to them. But one night while they were having dinner, a great halloing was heard outside, and when they went to the window, they saw Iscah's boys and their friends all staggeringly drunk outside the house. When the mob outside saw Lot's stern face at the window flanked by the shocked faces of the brethren, the sight was too much for them. They were incited to even more outrageous behavior and started to blow kisses and shout to the young men "Come into my arms, come into the garden, come into my bed" and "That one on the right is mine, my heart belongs to him" and all kinds of ridiculous and extravagant protestations of love. Really it would not have been so funny at all if Lot and the guests had not looked so horrified. But the girls started to giggle, and Leyla herself was almost bursting with laughter. Then Lot went outside, and his long face simply encouraged them to thumb their noses at him. He said sternly, "Don't you be so wicked" and, always one to labor the obvious, told them, "Such endearments should more properly be extended to young women," and then came the final outrage. He actually offered to send out the girls to them. Really, it was so humiliating, and the girls turned away with burning cheeks. Then the boys outside suddenly got disgusted and turned sober (they were never as drunk as they liked to pretend), and went off into the night.

It was shortly after this confrontation that Lot decided to leave Sodom. Of course, he couldn't just say that he had decided to pick up and leave because the moral climate didn't suit him. Oh no, that wasn't his style at all. He spent days alone closeted in his study and then finally emerged to announce self-importantly that the Lord had spoken to him. He had been told that both Sodom and Gomorrah had fallen into such decadence that God intended to destroy them. Lot was to take his family and flee the place immediately, not even stopping to pack or gather together their valuables.

The girls were torn between being pleased to leave a place where they had so little future and being annoyed that they had no warning and no chance to take their favorite possessions. As for Leyla, well. . . . She had never really liked the place to begin with, but somehow when it comes to leaving, it hurts a little to turn your back on a familiar spot, no matter how unhappy you've been in it.

She turned her back more easily on Sodom than Gomorrah. She thought of Iscah and the lads and all the good laughs they had had together, and she felt anxious for their safety. Even if God didn't destroy the towns as Lot said he would, it was fairly obvious that Nahor with his wild ways was set on a disastrous path. And what would become of Iscah in that case? The city fathers would be bound to blame her and upbraid her for her headstrong course in living alone. Of course, there was no way Leyla could intervene or help, but she could give a little moral support. And so, walking slowly and looking at Lot's inflexible back as he marched ahead, she slowed her step. "Gomorrah and Gomorrah and Gomorrah," she said beneath her breath, whispering the pretty name of the place like a charm. Lot had not even let her say good-bye to Iscah and the boys, and they would never know how she had hated leaving them. And pausing, she turned round for one last look at their city, hoping that on the skyline she might even catch a glimpse of their house. As she stood there, straining for one last look in their direction, it seemed that she could hear faintly the laughter and the music that always came from there. She wanted to cry out and tell Lot, for heaven's sake, to wait for her. But astonishingly, she found that her lips were frozen. She could no longer form the words, and her feet felt heavy and leaden. A great numbness was creeping from her toes through her feet and spreading over the whole of her body so that she was rooted to the ground. And still Lot and the girls went plodding ahead as if nothing in the world would stop them. . . .

The Lost Sheep

"One would not wish the members of our congregation to appear meddlesome and unneighborly," said the vicar.

"If you insist, Tom," he added as he accepted a glass of whiskey and soda from my father.

They often sat thus in the evening discussing church affairs, the vicar drinking whiskey and soda and my father gin and bitter lemon. Mostly they discussed financial matters. My father was an accountant, and having been asked to contribute his skills to the church, he had become chairman of the ways and means committee and the vicar's warden. My mother was pious and attended church out of a deep religious faith, but my father was not by nature devout, and I think now that he could not have been a believer. Still, he was more than willing to help with the practical side of parish life.

On this particular evening, however, they were not discussing finances. The vicar had said somberly when he entered the room that he wished for my father's advice on A Most Delicate Matter. His tone was enough to send me scuttling behind the couch, where, silent and unseen, I could hear everything that was said.

I already had an inkling of what was afoot. It concerned the unruly family that lived next door, separated from us only by the thin central wall that divided our semidetached houses. Astonishingly, three generations were now crowded into that tiny two-bedroom house. In the beginning there were Sam Assell and his wife, known as "the old couple" (I think they were prematurely aged), and their daughter, Winnie. Winnie was hugely, thyroidally overweight, with great dropsical legs. She was so vast and conspicuous when she walked abroad that the only simile ever used in the village for a fat person was "as big as Winnie Assell." It occurs to me, although I never formulated the thought until this moment, that whenever I hear of a thyroid condition or a case of elephantiasis, the image of Winnie Assell floats across the years as fresh and clear as if she lived next door to me today.

It was amazing that one of her colossal, misshapen bulk should have married, but then the whole family had a marked flair for the unlikely. It is not quite accurate to say that she married, since no formal ceremony was performed, but she did find a mate and he joined the ménage, all of them living together, drinking and brawling and carrying on in a way that violated every point in the unspoken but strict code of behavior that governed the village.

In due time and once more in the face of all reason and biological probability, Winnie, who still remained Assell, brought forth a son. She did so not in the least shamefacedly but with a proud air of defiance. Consistent with this pride, when the child was a few months old, the family acquired a huge perambulator, one of those elaborate baby carriages with great wheels and bouncy springs that seem fitted to be pushed by uniformed nannies in London parks, but which are otherwise absurdly cumbersome. No one else in the village had ever aspired to such splendor and it seemed outrageous that the fledgling and virtually fatherless Assell should be thus flaunted before them.

It was actually concerning this remarkable conveyance that the vicar and my father were in consultation. It had long since outgrown its usefulness as a baby carriage, and now in a much reduced, ramshackle condition it had been brought forth for the second phase of its career. It was presently being used by the Assells to transport their supply of booze from the Bull's Head Inn, which stood over by the church. A crisis had developed because the opening of the Bull's Head coincided roughly with the ending of the evening service on Sunday. Every Sunday for the past weeks the worshippers leaving the church to walk home had found themselves part of a procession led by Sam Assell and his heavily laden pram. Not only was the open display of bottles offensive to some members of the congregation, but Sam's own demeanor, jaunty and wobbling, strongly suggested insobriety. He was unconcerned by the waves of fury emanating from the procession in his wake, but the parishioners had formed a delegation and approached the vicar with a request that he Do Something.

"I don't condone Old Assell's way of life any more than the rest of the congregation do," said the vicar, "but a militant stance in the present instance seems to me very ill-advised."

"Quite so, Vicar," said my father, getting up to refill the glasses.

"I'm very reluctant to give offense to any villager," continued the vicar after a while. "The man isn't a member of the congregation at the present time, but I am not resigned to closing the door on him. I never abandon the possibility of such a person's joining us one day in our acts of worship."

"Quite," said my father, but in a very doubtful voice.

"Stranger things have happened," said the vicar. "One never knows what might bring about a change of heart. Times of distress and so on. . . . Well, my inclination is to offer up a prayer on his behalf during the evening service. What do you say to that, Tom?"

"Much the best course of action," said my father.

"I shall endeavor to persuade the vestry of the efficacy of prayer," said the vicar.

I was delighted, and all week long I looked forward to the prayer to stop Sam Assell bringing home booze in his pram. I tried to imagine what it would be like.

O Lord, prevent thy servant Sam from going to the Bull's Head.

O Lord, who sent down plagues of frogs and blains and boils on the Egyptian hordes, send now a few boils to stop Sam Assell. . . .

O Lord, who caused the gadarene swine to go helter-skelter off a cliff, cause Sam Assell and his pram to go over the bank of the Manchester Ship Canal. . . .

In the event, the prayer was a grave disappointment. It was utterly vague and did not even mention Sam Assell by name. The vicar merely spoke of those in our midst who had not yet been touched by the spirit of the Lord, and urged Him to pour down the light of His countenance upon them. I knew at once that it wouldn't work, and so did my mother. She said, "It'll take more than a prayer to sober that lot up."

As it happened, we were both wrong.

A week later when the vicar came to the house, my father beckoned him to the back window overlooking the Assells' yard. There, with all the broken chairs and abandoned bathroom fixtures, was the pram, one of its back wheels missing. Since the Assells were too feckless to mend anything, it was clear that the pram's period of usefulness had ended. Reduced to carrying his supplies in bags, Assell's progress was hampered, and his meeting with the churchgoers prevented.

"Looks like our prayers were answered," said my father.

"Ah, Tom," said the vicar, "more things are wrought by prayer than this world dreams on."

"Quite," said my father.

"Who knows but that one day the lost sheep himself might return to our fold?"

"Let's drink to that," said my father.

The prayer during the church service was discontinued, but it is possible that the vicar went on remembering Sam Assell in his own private prayers. I think he must have, for what else could account for his alacrity when he finally saw a way to bring Sam Assell into the fold.

The opportunity arose on the annual "Sunday-school treat," when the scholars were rewarded for their year's attendance by being taken on an outing in a charabanc (sharra-bang we called it), or sightseeing bus, to Blackpool. Blackpool was the nearest and most popular seaside town; it was the quintessential holiday resort, having, exactly as the brochures said, "something for everyone." There was a pier for fishing; a promenade for strolling; a good sandy beach for bathing, building castles, riding on donkeys, and watching Punch and Judy shows; and a pleasure ground with sideshows and games and whirligigs. I went to Blackpool for my holidays every summer, but in the autumn when the Sunday-school treat took place, there was something extra—the Great Blackpool Illuminations. There were arrangements of artificial lights strung up all over the town in an effort to prolong the tourist season and feather a little longer the nests of the local merchants. The lights were switched on ceremoniously by some famous personality like Vera Lynn or Terry Thomas or Wilfred

Pickles, and the whole town was transformed into a fairyland. After that, the lights were switched on all through the autumn as soon as it got dark, and the day-trippers had to stay on quite late to see the display. Our sharra drove us along the prom to see Snow White and the Seven Dwarfs and King John singing the Magna Carta before it headed back, taking us exhausted but not silenced, on the two-hour trip home.

At the end of one such giddy round of pleasure, I was standing by the coach, waiting for everyone to come back from the lavatories, when the vicar said to my father, "I believe the inviting light across the street is the window of a public house, Tom. Let us quickly fortify ourselves for the journey home. It is unlikely to be a peaceful journey."

"Not if it's anything like last year's," said my father. "I had a splitting head for three days afterwards."

And so they adjourned to the Star and Garter and left me sitting on the steps outside with a bottle of pop and a packet of Smith's Potato Crisps. What happened inside I heard my father tell my mother later.

They had no sooner got their drinks and settled down at a table when the vicar turned to my father and said, "Tom, is that not a familiar face on yonder bench?"

"Why, it's Sam Assell," said my father.

And sure enough there was Sam Assell, dead drunk and passed out on a bench in the Star and Garter.

"I bet he came on that trip from Nook Colliery that's already gone home," said my father.

"Surely," said the vicar, "they would not depart without ascertaining that no member of their group had gone astray?"

"Knowing that lot," said my father, "half of them could have gone astray, and the other half would be too far gone to notice."

"You astonish me," said the vicar, and for a while they drank in silence. At the end of a few minutes, the vicar said, "It is our obligation as Christians to see that our brother reaches his home in safety."

"He can't walk though," said my father.

"Then, Tom, we must carry him," said the vicar.

"I don't think we could manage that, just the two of us," said my father. What he really meant was that the vicar was too frail to carry any part of Sam Assell, drunk or sober.

"Then we must enlist the help of our driver," said the vicar.

The owner and driver of the charabanc was one Walter Rudd, an ill-humored and foul-mouthed man whose disposition was not improved by his nightly consumption of liquor. My father knew at once there was going to be trouble, but he could see there was no restraining the vicar from his good deed. They finished their drinks and returned to the coach.

"Walter Rudd isn't going to like this one bit," said my father.

"The good Walter," said the vicar, "is one of those who hides his kindness under a very rough exterior. Besides, he will be mollified when we pass around the hat."

It was the custom on these outings to take up a collection for the driver, and the vicar managed to effect Walter Rudd's cooperation by the promise of a particularly generous contribution to his tip.

"It's bad enough," said Walter Rudd, "carting this load of noisy buggers without throwing in a few drunks. Anybody that gets sick in this sharra cleans it up theirself."

All the same, he drove the coach to the front door of the Star and Garter, and carried out Sam Assell with the help of my father and the pub's bouncer (who was only too glad to get rid of one of his drunks so expeditiously), while the vicar hovered about, supervising the placing of Sam Assell on the back seat, and all the Sunday-school children cheered wildly.

And so we proceeded on our joyful, starlit return journey, my father and the vicar sitting on the front seat behind Walter Rudd and I in the seat behind them, licking a stick of Blackpool rock and listening.

"Our friend must realize at last who his true neighbors are," said the vicar. "Who knows but that this might be the turning point of his life! Miracles do sometimes still happen, Tom. Oh yes, miracles do happen."

He seemed very lit up about having Sam Assell in the back of the bus drunk. Actually, the real miracle was that Sam Assell slept all the way home, in spite of the deafening noise. The Sunday-school children were yelling chorus after chorus of

> She'll be coming round the mountain
> When she comes. . . .
>
> She'll be wearing silk pajamas
> When she comes. . . .

My father looked abashed on the vicar's account when they got to

> She'll be wearing khaki bloomers
> When she comes. . . .

But the vicar was thinking his own thoughts and smiling to himself. He woke up suddenly when they started singing, "Walter, Walter, lead me to the altar," and he leaned forward and tapped Walter Rudd on the shoulder and said, "No offense meant, my dear Walter, just the natural exuberance of the young after a day of pleasure."

"I'd belt the little buggers round their earholes if they was mine," said Walter Rudd.

"I'm sure our good Walter is a very indulgent parent," said the vicar to my father. I thought my father was going to laugh, but he just said, "I hope a few of them keep some voice for the early communion service."

"And if they don't," said the vicar, "the rest of us must try to be in good voice. It's only once a year, after all, Tom."

All the way home I nearly died from the suspense of wondering what the vicar would say to Winnie Assell when he took Sam home, and what Winnie Assell would say to the vicar. I thought it was the best Sunday-school trip I'd ever been on in my life.

It was very late when we finally got to the village and deposited all the Sunday-school children at certain prearranged spots. Walter Rudd was not very cheered up by the collection, yet he had no choice but to drive at last to Sam Assell's house if he wanted to get rid of him that night.

"I shall attempt to rouse the family," said the vicar. "No doubt Sam's son-in-law will assist us in carrying our brother to his home." I slipped off the bus before my father could stop me and stood at the Assell's doorstep while the vicar knocked.

At first he rapped very gently with his hand on the door, but there was no answer. Finally, he was obliged to use the knocker and knock so hard that the noise echoed up and down the street. There was still no sound inside, and the vicar said, "The Assell family seem to be remarkably sound sleepers. I suppose liberal amounts of beer induce such habits."

He started knocking again, and suddenly the window of the house on the other side shot up, and Mrs. Bessie Brand, her hair all done up in curlers and white papers, stuck her head out. She mustn't have noticed the vicar because she yelled, "Stop yer bloody din at this time o'night. Yer could knock the bloody door down, and they wouldn't 'ear yer. They've all gone to Blackpool for a week's holiday."

It was impossible to tell whether the language or the information caused the vicar the most pain, but a very sorrowful expression crossed his face, and he took out a big handkerchief and wiped his forehead with it.

He walked back to the coach and said, "Tom, the situation is a little more complicated than one originally surmised."

At this point our front door opened, and my mother yanked me inside and off to bed before I could hear the rest.

The next morning after matins I was in the vestry waiting for my father to finish counting the offertory money. The vicar said, "You'll be pleased to hear, Tom, that our friend seemed none the worse this morning for his little misadventure. He spent the night on the daybed in my library, and the good Mrs. Hope prepared a most ample breakfast for him this morning. I arranged for him then to be driven to the station in Atherton, whence he caught the Blackpool train to rejoin his family and resume his holiday. I furnished his train fare and gave him a five-pound note in addition."

"We could take the money out of the foreign missions box, Vicar," said my father. "The donations have been quite generous lately."

"That could not be justified, Tom," said the vicar. "The error was largely my own, and I feel I should make the amends."

"Did he thank you?" asked my father.

"Alas no," said the vicar. "I believe he regarded the attempt to assist him as unwarranted meddling."

"He had a point, Vicar," said my father with a smile.

"Oh indeed, indeed," said the vicar. "One's zeal exceeded one's caution in this instance."

I waited to hear some gnomic wisdom or some hopeful prognostication about God's working in mysterious ways or about His mills grinding slowly, but none came. I think the vicar had given up on Sam Assell.

I guessed as much, but I never knew for sure because shortly afterward the vicar accepted the call to another parish in the south of England. When he came for a farewell drink at our house, he told my father, "I'm too old for this ministry, Tom. A younger man is needed and perhaps one more at home with the people of Lancashire. I'm West Country, you know, and I've always felt myself on foreign soil here."

"A little too rough, Vicar?" asked my father.

"Rough, yes," said the vicar, "but then one learns to look for the good qualities under the rough surface. I shall miss you, Tom. You must be sure and call on me if you ever find yourself in the vicinity of Devon."

It was several years later, while we were on a summer holiday in Devon, that we decided to look up the vicar. Actually, I was the one who wanted to see him. I no longer went to church at all, but I was going to the university the next year to study English. I had this feeling that it was the vicar who first got me interested in language, and I wanted to hear his precise southern speech again and tell him that I had been much influenced by him.

Unfortunately, the years had not treated him well. He had become senile, and it was impossible to communicate with him properly. He kept asking the same questions repeatedly and forgetting the answers.

"Tell me, Tom," he said, "how is that old renegade who lived next door to you?"

"Sam Assell?" said my father. "Not very well, Vicar. In fact, he passed on some years ago."

And then again, later: "And Sam Assell, the old sinner? Does he still go about unscathed, or have his sins caught up with him at last?"

"Well," said my father, "he passed away some time back."

"Ah, you see, Tom," said the vicar, "the Lord is not flouted."

"Well, he was a good age, Vicar," said my father. "He lived to be nearly eighty and went very peacefully in his sleep one night."

Just as we were leaving, the vicar called us back and once more, "While I remember, Tom. Whatever became of your old neighbor, Sam Assell? Has he abandoned his wild ways?"

"I hope so, Vicar," said my father. "He was called to his Maker some years ago."

A Climate of Extremes

Before I came to this city, I didn't think much about what it would be like. I was offered a job, and it paid well. But just before I traveled out, I was in Vancouver with a group of people, having drinks in a garden overlooking the bay. It was a wonderful view. There was a woman in the crowd from here, and I remember she said, "I'm drinking up all this beauty, because there isn't any on the prairies." Then the others all made jokes, the way they do. "Oh, come on, Jenny, flat is beautiful."

Afterward, they talked seriously, some of them, about the beauty of the prairies. They described sundogs; the effect of rowanberries against the snow; sunsets all aflame with the color of flamingos; snow trimmed neat and artificial, like the icing on a wedding cake; hoarfrost on the trees turning the whole city into a stage set for *Swan Lake.* But all the same, that woman alarmed me. There was such a hunger in her voice, such a yearning. It was like hearing a deprived person who says she's never in her life had a square meal or a soft bed or a decent stitch of clothing. And means it. It frightens you to hear that.

So anyway, I came out here to teach. It was a lot different then. Much bleaker than it is now. Two of the college buildings were up, but there was no landscaping, and they just sat there, big and square, looking sort of marooned in a big patch of mud. Gumbo, they call it. The clayey soil that sticks to your shoes. There were a few apartment buildings — not many, just one or two — and they sat in big patches of concrete. The natives boast that every single tree in the town has been planted by hand. But I couldn't get used to things not growing. All my life I'd lived where trees and flowers grew naturally. I'd taken them quite for granted.

At first I consoled myself by getting plants in pots. Every day I went out searching for them. Any plants that were leafy and flowery and scented. They have hyacinths in the shops for Valentine's Day. I got a lot of them. White ones. The white ones have the strongest smell always. That's because they can't attract bees in cther ways, and so they compensate for not having bright colors.

I think many feel the way I did. You only have to look at the offices at the university. The people don't just hang up a plant or two, here and there. They're fanatical. They go wild and turn the place into jungles. There are hanging baskets all over the ceilings, plants sprouting in the windows and rampaging all over the tables. They aren't trimmed in the least, and put out tendrils and ramifications that curl around the furniture. Sometimes they have prickles and thorns that hook on to visitors. Cactuses, Crowns of Thorns, and Rosary Plants come cascading down the bookshelves. And people talk about what's normal! Anyway, these ones with the jungle-offices are extremists. This is a climate of extremes, and those who live in it tend to be excessive in many ways. In gardening they are.

But the curious thing is, I couldn't grow anything. I got plants and watered and sprayed and fed them, but every single one curled up and died. They were doomed. I would have liked a jungle-office with ivies wreathing about and spider plants propagating and hibiscuses sticking out their . . . proboscises, I think you call them. But nothing lived. People sympathized and tried to understand. They said it was too dry for this and that. Gardenias need moisture. They need acid soil. They need more sun. They get frostbitten when you carry them from the flower shop. Try feeding them. Try giving them distilled water. It wasn't any good.

Well, after awhile I got a house with a little garden. You know how the houses are here. So close together. I could look right from my kitchen window into my neighbor's kitchen and see what he was having for breakfast. Shreddies, Fruit Loops, and so on. All that space around the city, but the houses inside the city squeezed up so tight together.

All my neighbors were gardeners. I've never seen people garden the way they do here. They work at it with grim determination, as if to prove some hypothesis in the teeth of all reasonable evidence — fanatically, obsessively, compulsively. Everywhere else even keen gardeners just water, transplant a few things, perhaps buy bedding plants, annuals. But the prairie winter kills most things, and every summer the people have to start from scratch. They get earth first, then peat and topsoil. Then they stick all the flowers in the soil. Petunias, zinnias, marigolds. If they have window boxes, they have geraniums going up, trailing vines hanging down, and little shrubs leafing out in all directions. I have one neighbor that grows seeds in his basement under fluorescent lights in the winter. As soon as it gets warm in June, he brings out the shoots for some natural light and sun, and they start to grow and grow. And then later he makes his garden. One day you go by, and the garden has taken place that very afternoon. And all summer long it blooms and blooms, so bright and cheerful. Then in the fall, after the first frost, he clears it all away. Pulls up all the plants and throws them in a rubbish heap, and there it is. The garden's over.

Well, I couldn't grow anything in my garden. They said the pine trees made the soil too acid and too shady and dropped things — needles, pine cones, some sort of resinous sap. I tried shade-loving perennials, but they didn't love that much shade and they loathed the pine cones and needles and resin. I never could get the right combination anywhere. So I had a company come in and lay concrete in one half of the yard and gravel in the other. The neighbors thought it quite a joke. They said, "Why not set parking meters in the concrete and make something out of it. Or put tombstones in the gravel and an urn here and there. Gussy the place up, why don't you!"

I was lonely, too, because the inhabitants of this place seemed like strangers to me. I am a pale person, thin-skinned, while the natives of these plains are tough and weather-beaten. Generations of their ancestors have weathered the prairie winters, and this is their blood's country. They're like huskies, who, when they sense an on-coming blizzard, sniff the air in an ecstasy of anticipation. They tell stories of earlier storms and hard times and daring adventures they've survived.

Even the newcomers, by imitation, develop the same hardiness. They say, boasting a little, "I consider it a challenge to live here." And they give advice on how to endure and be happy. "Take up curling. Get yourself some snowshoes. Breed huskies. They amply reward you for all the trouble. Learn to ski. Cross-country is safer than downhill, and more invigorating. Get outdoors in the cold. It's healthy. Kills off all the germs and only some of the people. Ha ha ha."

I couldn't be convinced. I hated those snarling, half-savage dogs. The pitiless prairie winds flayed my cheeks. So, I stayed indoors looking out at the whiteness and thinking: Somewhere roses are blooming. At last they grew irritated. I was a living denial of their most cherished belief that these prairies are habitable. They lost patience at last and said, "Oh well be miserable then," and I was left alone.

That was when it started. I had this old school friend, Sandra Wentworth. Yes, the same name as I. When we were younger, everyone called us "The Two Sandras," though in fact our names were different. Her mother was a royalist and named her Alexandra. Mine named me Cassandra for an astrologer who cast horoscopes for the *Daily Mail.* Anyway, for years I've written to Sandra every Sunday of my life. I do it on Sunday because that was the day in school when we were obliged to write home, and we kept up the habit. We've done it for over forty years. She married, you see, and owns a big house in Kew. That's outside London, and she has an interesting life, doing lots of things. They're always going to galleries and shows and concerts — Covent Garden, Royal Albert Hall, command performances. She describes everything to me. All the men in evening dress, and the women gowned and coiffed and jeweled, and everyone so sparkling with light and life it's unbelievable.

So, with needing to write and missing a garden so much, one day I told her that I had found a house with four acres of land around it, four huge city lots, and wondered what to do with it. I thought I would make a kind of park and go in seriously for gardening and landscaping. Did she believe me? Why of course she did. People in England never question what you tell them about Canada. You could say anything. Before I came out here, someone told me the prairies come right to the edge of the city. You know what I imagined? I imagined hills or mountains with clefts and ridges coming right to the edge of the town. I imagined getting out through gulleys and valleys. You could tell people you saw a moose going down the street, and they'd just think: Well, a moose. How interesting. That's Canada for you. When my father was in India, he met a tiger walking down the street one day. Amazing what you see abroad.

For them, Canada is Elsewhere and Abroad and full of Foreigners. Anything can happen. Thus, the gardening started. It was a means of keeping my sanity, of not losing my mind.

No, it was not just a product of my imagination. I can't invent anything. I'm quite literal-minded in certain ways. It was more an exercise of memory than of imagination. You see, all my early life I lived in such lovely places. I have the most wonderful memories. I remember as a girl going to spend the Easter holidays with an aunt in the country. She had a great, ample house in its own grounds. That was what they called the garden — "the grounds." There was a man whose job was just to maintain the grounds. That was what he was called. Never the gardener for some reason. Maybe they were socially sensitive or something. I remember the days there. The orchard all filled with daffodils. And narcissi, pheasant-eye narcissi, white flowers with little centers like the eyes of pheasants. Yes. That's why they were called that. On long, slender, green stems. The whole field full of them. And cowslips and violets and bluebells, all smelling so sweet that the scent floated on the air like music. And the sound of cuckoos in the distance, very muted and soft. I liked that wild part of the garden. But there were formal gardens too. Herbaceous borders and rose gardens with paths and walks and statuary here and there.

So all one winter long I worked on this garden, reconstructing it in every detail on my acres of land and describing it in my letters to Sandra. I had to think it all out very carefully and write notes and make plans. Remembering exactly. That was hard work. How hard it was. For instance, there was a sundial with an inscription on it. But I couldn't for the life of me recall what that inscription was. I'd close my eyes and concentrate. I'd walk down the path and bring myself gradually to the spot, and it would always be the same — blank. For days I was irritable, nervous, almost frantic at last. And then, one night, right in the middle of the night, I woke with a start. I sat up in bed and knew what it was: TEMPUS FUGIT. Well, yes. It's laughable really. So obvious. I might have guessed. But it had gone out of my mind so completely — yet I got it back. You know, that gives you satisfaction. To think that things in life, in the past, are not lost completely, that if you think hard enough you can get them back.

And Sandra loved it. She wrote of how they waited for the postman to bring my letters, and how they longed to hear more about the garden. They envied me, she said, because it was hard to grow things satisfactorily where they were. She said there was so much rain that everything was stunted and behind. She said the climate seemed to be getting worse. Clive swore it was. Clive's her husband. They wanted me to send snapshots, but I said that wouldn't do justice to the riot of color in the garden. That was quite true. The colors would have been false, as in those nasty Kodachrome snapshots of flower gardens. They're all wrong. Too highly colored, like technicolor movies. They never catch the subtlety of the shades, of the nuances. And black and white certainly wouldn't have given the right effect. She could quite understand that. Besides, I don't own a camera.

Well, it was very hard work, but it was rewarding in its own way. And so, after I had done the orchard with the apple trees and wild flowers, the herbaceous borders and the rose garden, I needed a new project. Guess what I decided to do? I decided to put in a pool. No, an actual swimming pool. No, I don't swim, but this was to be a pool to sit around. No. I told you already, nothing was invented. This is the whole point. This was a pool from a place I visited once in Texas. You see, people are very hospitable in Texas. You go to a meeting there and talk to the natives, and they say, "What! Stopping at the Holiday Inn? What nonsense is this! You're in Texas now. Yes Ma'am." And before you know it, they have your luggage collected, and you're checking out of the Holiday Inn and unpacking in their guest room or in their guest house. And they're telling the help, "Take good care of her. We've grown mighty fond of this little lady."

They have such lovely places. But the really hard part of this garden was that I wasn't ever in the Texas places long enough to remember them easily. I was there more recently than at Rosemount, that's my aunt's home, but not as long. And another thing is that early memories are more vivid than later ones. And the more recent memories are the faintest of all. For these reasons this part of the garden was very difficult indeed.

One Texas house was a ranch house with gardens on all sides. They have ranch houses with galleries on every side so that a person can walk outdoors from room to room and still be shaded from the heat of the sun. That's what they tell you. To recreate the garden of this house was my summer project. I began it when classes ended in April, and it had to be finished by fall. Why? For a number of reasons. I should have thought they were obvious. You can't do much here in the winter. The contractors can't work then. And also, I like to do things on time. I work by a schedule. I'm really a very organized person, in my work and everything I do.

Well, there was a tennis court on one side of the ranch house, but I didn't intend to put a tennis court in my garden, because I don't play. Also, it's a lot of work keeping up a court. The pool? Well, that was different because, although it was a swimming pool, the visual effect was the main thing. It was a kidney-shaped pool, pleasant to sit around in summer and agreeable to look at in winter. I put in long French windows and made the room overlooking the pool blend in with it. The garden was full of crepe myrtles and oleanders and mesquites, and in the distance there were live oaks, and the mourning doves in them purred and murmured all day long in the heat. That memory is quite fresh. It was so hot that when you looked out, the whole landscape swam and floated. But the sound of the doves was soothing. And the scents of the oleanders and the crepe myrtles were sweet like vanilla. And the sitting room in the house was as cool as a vault, and — this is the striking thing about it — every single piece of furniture or fabric was apple-green. Green velvet chairs, green satin draperies, green carpeting under your feet. Even the white marble tables took on a greenish cast. It was like moving and breathing in a strange medium in which all the shapes and colors were transmuted. Unreal, in a way, subterranean, and yet not at all unpleasant. And cool, it was so cool.

Around the pool outside they had set plants from even hotter and more exotic regions — palm trees and palmettos and retamas and jujube trees with fruit like dates. Perhaps they *were* dates. I asked very particularly about everything when I was there. And so I recalled it and could put it in my own garden that I was planning and arranging all that summer.

I suppose it was a bizarre idea. All those tropical plants in such a cold climate. I grant that it was eccentric. But then everyone has some eccentricity. When I was growing up in a small mining village in the north of England, it was incredible how many unusual people there were. They were quite accepted, and even liked. I remember one old woman called Mrs. Gallimore. They called her Galli-curci. Well, there was this bus service that ran from our village to the next with a really strict schedule. You could set the clock on the mantle-piece by it. It arrived on the hour at the market square in the next town and left at a certain time, and arrived at the Bull's Head in our village at a certain time. There was a ten minute wait at each end, and you sat and read the signs in the bus. There were signs, and the school children picked away the letters, so they read FLEAS KEEP YOUR FEET OFF THE EATS and NO S ITTING and so on. . . . Well, this woman, Mrs. Gallimore, rode the bus all day long, from morning to night, every single day. I don't remember the details—if she paid, when she ate, and when she went to the bathroom. But I remember that she chatted to everyone. That was at first. Then later she started smelling. People noticed that it was unpleasant to be near her. But it was still a joke. Not a cruel joke. This is hard to explain, but these people were just local characters and accepted. That was why she was called Galli-curci, because she began to hum. That means she got a bit whiffy. Then it got really strong . . . really bad in the whole bus. An old woman driven crazy by loneliness or grief. I don't know what it was exactly. Perhaps she lost a son in the war. Many did. Or perhaps she never had a son in the first place. Who can calculate the amount of grief necessary to push a person to extremes? I don't remember at all what happened. I don't like to dwell on unpleasant things. People can be so cruel. So heartless. But I like to give pleasure.

And so, the garden. It was giving my friend so much pleasure. Immense pleasure. That was her actual phrase. "Clive and I got *immense pleasure* from your account. . . ."

Indeed, for a long time I assumed that it was entirely on Sandra's account that I was creating gardens. I even felt a certain pride in my altruism. I suppose that was smug and self-satisfied, like those robust women who come knocking at your door. "This is Heart Week. And I'm collecting for the Heart Fund." They have fur coats and silk scarves and unassailable hearts. Their entire stance says: This is something I am doing for less fortunate human beings than myself. Well, the recognition was forced upon me at last that I too was one of the self-righteous. It happened long before the final disaster and came about as a result of Sandra's death.

Yes, I learned of the death when a neighbor wrote to say that Sandra had passed away. The neighbor? Well, there was no one else to write. Sandra lived alone I discovered. I don't know whether her husband had died or not. I never met him and knew nothing of him. Perhaps he died years ago, and she failed to mention the fact. It is sometimes very difficult to speak of troubles when one is in the midst of them. Perhaps he never even existed at all. The neighbor simply said that Sandra had passed away and that her passing was in many ways a blessing. She had been in frail health for many years and had been unable to go out at all. She remained always in her room in a cheap boardinghouse — Holly Lodge in Kew. I think I mentioned that before. *In reduced circumstances.* That was how the neighbor described her life. She said she lived *in reduced circumstances.*

So by the time the catastrophe happened, I had already accepted this one basic fact: that whatever my motivation was in the beginning, I was now working for myself alone. I welcomed the knowledge of my own selfishness and planned accordingly.

Reveling in my newly discovered freedom, I was carried on to a higher plateau of happiness. I envisaged a new life of absolutely uninhibited gardening in which I could do anything at all that I desired. At last I could plan something suited only to my own taste. *Coepit Vita Nuova.*

I conceived at once the idea of a purely white garden. I had seen such gardens in various places. One I saw in the Deep South, the garden of an old plantation home along the Natchez Trace. It was full of camellias, gardenias, and azaleas, all tropical, fragrant, exotic, and completely white. In England too I had seen a white garden, in the grounds of a castle in the Kentish weald. There the flowers were not tropical. They were the humdrum flowers of an or-

dinary English cottage garden — cabbage roses, foxgloves, Canterbury bells, and daisies. Though there were also arum lilies, furled
about their central stamens like veils around young brides. How
serenely beautiful they were. I intended to combine the plants from
the tropical and the temperate climes in a riot of bloom and scent.
Gardenias would jostle lilies of the valley, rambling roses would
cascade from their trellises and their petals fall among the oleanders
and the dogwood blossoms. I was exultant, reveling for the first time
in the excesses of my own imagination.

It was at this precise moment that the ferret-faced man appeared
on my doormat. I can see him now, rooted there, like some noxious
outgrowth burgeoning from the very earth itself. His warty face was
terra cotta from being seared by wind and sun, his body paunchy and
misshapen from his gorgings and swillings in beer parlors and other
troughs. A cap, stuck firm on his head like a lid screwed down tight
on a jar, announced the name of a branch of farm implements. He
wore a bright red jacket to discourage hunters from mistaking him
for a four-legged beast and shooting on sight, and under that a soiled
undershirt printed with another slogan, as if his only use for literacy
was to announce the names of those who supplied the ammunition
for his dreary trade:

PRAIRIE PESTICIDES
WESTERN COMBINES AND TRACTORS
SASKATCHEWAN FERTILIZERS INCORP.

From beneath his faded denim trousers he flung out laced boots with
thick crepe soles that afforded him a surer purchase on the ground
when he walked to and fro on it.

At once he began to utter, spouting explanations of his treacherous
purpose. He said he had a son. I never doubted it for a minute. Don't
his kind ever spawn indiscriminately, breeding and reproducing over
the whole world? His son had a wife. One might have guessed. The
wife was about to have a child. I knew it almost before he said the
word. Oh the endless dreariness, the rampaging energy and disorder
of it all. And what did he want from me? Simply my space. He
wished to take it from me. He said he owned the house. He spoke of
rent and leases and foreclosures and renewals and lawyers, burbling

on in a language I did not understand and in a voice I could not bear to listen to. It needed oiling like the farm machinery, the names of whose manufacturers he so proudly flaunted.

No, I did not try to reason with him. There is no way to talk to his kind — the earthy, literal-minded clods, rooted in the mundane. How could I have urged my claim, my stake in the place? My rights were the memories, the creations, the fantasies that needed roots in one place as surely as his incautiously propagating species. But I could not defend these rights against the growing, reproducing army of his progeny. They were alive — heavy-breathers, greedy-eaters, glandular and pig-like in their cunning and monstrosity. The very words discriminated against me. Everything I valued was defined as something it was not, intangible, invisible, impalpable, incorporeal. I felt as if I were confronted with some grotesque Samson, bracing himself on his hind legs to pull down my trellises, my gazebos, my dovecotes, to trample my flowers, my wrens' nests, my frail vines. It was an unfair battle. I could not fight on his terms, and I refused to try. I quietly bade him good day and waved him away.

Oh, but I was not helpless. Have I not always made my own accommodations, adjustments? The mind has its own force and never more so than when it needs to fight and plans a rear-guard action. I summoned all the resources in my power to defeat his purpose. It was then that I decided to burn down the house.

It was not, of course, difficult. Getting rid of things never is, you know. The bedroom where I work is a bare room, since I am by nature ascetic. There are no curtains, only the narrow slats of venetian blinds. My desk is a plain, unpainted pine. Beside my desk is a wicker wastebasket, half filled with papers and with shavings from the pencil sharpener. Beside the desk is my narrow bed with its few light covers — the white pillow and the Hudson Bay blanket with its broad stripes, the only bands of color in the room. My robe lies across the bed — a gray flannel gown with a cowl. Over my bed is a convex Victorian mirror that holds the room in a globe.

I sat at my desk and lit the matches and dropped them one by one into the wastebasket. The whole box. Those matches with wooden stems. I like the smell of the phosphorous when the matches strike on the side of the box. One by one I dropped them into the basket. I love matches and matchboxes. When I was a child, I spent hours making dollhouse furniture from them. I thought of that, dropping the lighted matches into the basket. It took about ten minutes — first the paper caught and then the shavings and then the wicker. It made a fine blaze and burned so bright and cheerful. The sides of my legs began to feel scorched. They used to feel so when long ago I toasted bread by holding it on a brass fork over the open coals. I loved that scorching, but when it became too hot I moved to the bed and stretched out upon it.

I was not afraid. You read about people being burned at the stake, and it makes you shiver. But it is only horrible for the spectators. For the victim, attuned to her own voices, it is not so. There are protections against physical suffering. This is what I believe. Before the flesh is seared and the bone charred, the smoke mercifully annihilates and the consciousness fades.

And so, lying on my bed in the warm, bright room, with my eyes closed, I was happy. My lids did not keep out completely the red glow of the flames. It was like lying on a beach in the midday sun. I remembered a holiday that I once spent in Italy. The Ligurian coast was very hot that summer. I lay on the beach all day, and the sun beat down terrifically. The sand was so warm that it was painful to the soles of the feet, and no green trees provided shade. The luxury hotels that bounded the beach on one side were all concrete and blaring music. I closed my eyes against the glare, and my ears against the beat of the music. The incoming tide pounded the seawall incessantly. I listened to the roaring of the incoming tide. It roared and roared in my ears until at last, listening to it, I drifted into a profound and peaceful sleep.

Laocoön, My Father

Three nights ago I dreamed again of Laocoön, my father. I knew then that it would never end. I thought at first that after five years I should forget. When we talked of disasters, he told me that was how long it took to recover. I remember asking once when we spoke of Tiresias's blindness and Hector's shameful death. I took my father's words quite literally, perhaps too literally I think now. I had asked curiously when I watched Hecuba mourning for Hector, "When will she be well again?" He never liked Hecuba, and he said, with a look of scorn, "Oh, her. She'll be over it by this time tomorrow. For anyone else it would take five years." He thought she was silly and self-indulgent, and perhaps she was.

We spoke often of the royal family, for I was inordinately proud of our connection. When I saw them, all those handsome, well-dressed people, walking on the battlements of the city, my heart turned over. In conversations with my friends, I found ways of slipping in references to my cousin Helen or my cousin Creusa. I was even proud of my cousin Cassandra with her mad look. She was as handsome as the others but farouche somehow, with unruly hair falling all over her head and shoulders in elflocks and tendrils. It was not that she was careless in dressing her hair, but she shook her head so much, tossing it like a wild horse, that the locks fell from their bindings. My mother said, "They'll be doing alright if they ever find a husband for that one." My father looked as if he could have strangled her but caught himself. He did his best to avoid quarrels with my mother, but he liked Cassandra best of them all for some reason, and he hated

Helen. He thought she was dangerous. "An irresponsible woman," he said. "A trouble-maker."

I loved her even more after I came to Greece with her, and I wished my father had liked her more in the early days, those far-off times. When I think back on them, though, I feel as if my innocence was false, like a deliberate blindness. It was as if I was poised on the rim of a tank of man-eating eels, hardly noticing the seething below the surface but trailing my hand idly across the water, thinking how serene and peaceful everything is, was, will be, was, is, will be.

But it ended quite suddenly. I could never remember how my father died or what happened to my mother and my brothers. There was so much confusion, so much fighting and killing and death and burning. I care less about what happened to my mother and brothers than to him, for truly I was my father's daughter. My brothers were crude — always playing soldiers, staging battles, and tormenting animals. My mother was not crude exactly, but she was silly, forever rattling on about matters of no importance and no interest. My father hardly listened to what she said, nor did I. But I listened to everything he said and remembered a great deal of it, for he was a wise man. I guessed they killed him with one of their long knives. I thought about him as I did my chores, and it made me ache, even when I was so content to be near her. When I picked up her scattered garments, I pressed my face into them and breathed her smells — all flowery like olive oil and orange blossom.

The other day something happened. I was in her room, picking up this and that and thinking my own thoughts, when I looked up suddenly and there she was, lurking in the doorway, watching me with that furtive expression of hers. I was close enough to see the hairs on her upper lip and the black eyebrows meeting in the middle and the strangely pale skin and the deep, dark eyes. "A dangerous woman and ruthless," my father said. Then, smiling mockingly, she went swiftly away, and I went to my room. I lay down hot with the memory of her and her closeness, my hands doing what she had not done but what I wanted her to do, parting my lips and breathing very heavily. Then, in the heat, I fell asleep and dreamed so happy and contented of that other time. Always the same dream — the three of us sitting on the rim of an ornamental pool, looking at the dragonflies skimming, the kingfishers darting. And yet, we never did sit together like that, my father, Helen, and I.

Then suddenly I woke to my loss again. Many people in that other place blamed her for all our trouble, but I didn't. They spoke of her leading Paris into bad ways, leading him on. But she didn't need to lead anyone on: she was, and is, so beautiful that no one could help loving her. Except my father, that is. "A mannish woman," he said, "bold and degenerate." I suppose she is like a man in many ways, and she looked even more so beside Paris. They were a funny pair — she tall, muscular, dark, and flat-chested; he pale and slightly built like a stripling.

The fact was, Paris was shy with women, and it took someone like Helen to captivate him. And to tell the truth, for all the difficulties, it was a great relief to his family and friends. It's an embarrassment when the king's son is always besotted over some slave boy, and the servants go about whispering and calling him "the princess" and "the vestal virgin" behind his back. You can go on for so long saying "He'll get over it in a few years," and then you begin to wonder. My father blamed Hecuba for making such a pet of him and molly-coddling him. So when he fell for Helen and nothing would do but he must bring her with him out of Greece and into Troy, they all said he was a dark horse and a real tiger when he was aroused, and he just had to find the right woman, and then . . . well, they rolled their eyes as if there were no words adequate to describe the wild orgies that ensued. Which was quite ridiculous in Paris's case. And then to add to this confusion of family pride and anxiety, the hostility toward the Greeks got into it. The idea that the wife of King Menelaus had taken a fancy to one of Priam's sons fed the Trojan appetite for sensation and their national pride. And there it was, as simple as that. But not so simple to undo all the trouble it caused. Not that he wasn't carried away by Helen. He was mesmerized by her, anyone could see that. When his eyes fell on her, they lighted up with a mixture of fascination and, I think, fear as well. He seemed a little afraid of her, but she handled him well. She genuinely liked him and she treated him tenderly, as if he were fragile; she amused him with her uninhibited manner and her extravagant, careless way with clothes. She was quite glamorous, and he played for hours with her brooches and pins and robes. I often wonder what happened to him when Helen came back with Menelaus. I expect he was killed with all the others. Poor Paris, I'm sure he didn't die bravely.

I used to wish I could talk to her and ask what happened in those last days of Troy. One of my persistent waking daydreams was that we were lying together, she and I, and she was answering all my questions—What happened to the twins? What happened to my cousins, Priam and Hecuba and Cassandra? And what happened to Laocoön, my father? But she has always kept me at a distance in this place and never spoken to me much. I thought at first it was because of my rank as a slave, but I wonder sometimes if she thinks I remember too much. She would be surprised at how little I remember. Even the people and events I used to remember have become jumbled, so that I no longer know which are dreams and which are memories. To speak truly, I have suspected for a long time that I am a little mad. Yet they have been kind to me here. They gave me a little room—well it's an alcove really, but with a soft bed—and there has always been enough to eat. And if there wasn't enough, there was so much food left lying around Helen's room that I could feed on that—bread and fruit and even wine, goblets half full of delicious, heady wine. My father was quite right when he told the Trojans long ago that the Greeks were not savage animals. The people of Troy were lazy, my father said. They refused to build or work or make any effort whatsoever to keep up the city and improve it. The streets were crumbling with neglect, and the temples were falling into disrepair. They said to him, "Why should we keep things up when the Greeks are at our gates and disaster is imminent?"

"We are mortal," he said, "and disaster is always imminent."

"But Laocoön," they said, "not on such a scale as this. If the Greeks enter the city, they will tear us limb from limb, feed us to lions and eels, cook us in stews with toads and rats, burn us and everything they find."

"Nonsense," my father said, "they are men like ourselves."

"And women like ourselves," said Cassandra with that maniacal laugh of hers.

"Aye, women too, like our women no doubt," said my father. Cassandra could always make him smile.

"If there is a battle, they may not win. If they win, they may not destroy everything. And what is the alternative anyway? If we build things and they tear them down, they will have destroyed the work of our days and hands, that's true. But if we build nothing, we shall have defeated ourselves, which is more ignoble and impious."

So spoke Laocoön, my father. But the people called him "gloom-pot" and "misery" and went off with resentful, backward glances to idle along the walls staring at the Greek tents.

My mother said to him, "Why do you have to keep annoying people? You'll never change them or get them to change their ways, you should know that by now. And how will she ever find a husband when we have no friends, and you make yourself more and more unpopular?" I wanted to protest that I could find my own husband. My father looked furious, but after awhile he simply said, in a reasonable voice, "Well you, my dear, are not unpopular, far from it."

This last was true. My mother insinuated herself everywhere and especially into the royal palace. She carried gossip and gifts of sweets to Hecuba, who was greedy and acquisitive. And when Hecuba came to our house and admired a piece of furniture or a vase in that pointed, hinting way she had, my mother was quick to offer it to her as a gift and to look gratified when the old queen accepted it. She endeared herself to the younger members also. She helped Paris with the needlework he liked to do, and she helped Helen in the endless task of brushing and dressing her long hair. "An indolent, vain woman," my father said Helen was. In some ways he was right. Helen could sit for hours just gazing raptly at her own reflection, while someone stood and brushed her hair. My mother, in her efforts to ingratiate herself even to the least influential member of the royal family, offered to do this task and performed it quite happily whenever Helen agreed to let her do it. And I, as a slave, have had to do it whenever I am bidden.

And so I stood, brushing her hair, last night, when my whole life changed again. Helen was always silent at these times, and I was often in a trance of happiness, looking at her lovely face and tending her needs. "A pampered, spoiled woman," my father said. Yet, when she stared at herself, she didn't look self-satisfied or even much interested in what she saw. It was hard to know what she was thinking, for she too must have had troubled and confusing thoughts. I wondered if she also had difficulty remembering her life in Troy and knowing what happened and what she had simply imagined, but I never dared to ask.

"A mischief-maker and a fermenter of strife," my father called her. It is true she was always at the center of strife. But she never exerted herself to cause trouble, it just came to her naturally. She is like some beautiful statue that we all, men and women, clothe and animate with our own imaginings and with all the hopes for the fulfilment of our little lives. Perhaps, now that I think of it, that kind of person is the most dangerous kind of all. It must be a great burden to be such a one. No wonder that she holds herself aloof and says so little.

I do not know how long we had been thus, last night, for time is suspended when I dress her hair. It was growing dark, shadows were gathering, and only little vessels of oil, with small flames at their lips, made spots of light about the room. From time to time her head fell forward with a jerk and we both started. She shook her head and seemed to wake up, and then she steadied her fixed stare at herself and we continued as before.

The brushing deepened our trance, but suddenly one of the lamps, which she must have set too precariously on the edge of the window-sill, fell to the floor with a tinkling sound. We both woke instantly and turned and saw the oil spill, and before either of us could move to pick it up, the flame blazed up and the oil caught fire and the fire spread to the heaps of Helen's robes lying scattered about the floor where she had lately stepped out of them. "An untidy woman. A slattern with disorderly habits," my father said of her, though that was no time to be thinking of it. We both flinched against the wall as the clothes, burning up fast and furious, sealed us off in our side of the room behind a huge and growing curtain of flame. Helen and I together, caught once more in a great conflagration.

And, wonderful to tell, it was that curtain of fire that destroyed the other curtain in my mind that had shut off all the memories of the end of Troy and of my coming here to Greece. This last catastrophe uncovered that other buried one.

I remembered then that Helen and I had cowered thus, hiding in the temple while noise and confusion and fighting and killing went on all around us. We listened to the voices raising the alarm and to the running footsteps, catching our breath when the footsteps and clanging weapons drew near, letting it out again each time the steps passed by and left us unmolested. And in that time, fear and dread put us out of our daylight minds, and we became like animals hiding in the ground, clinging together and trying to merge and lose ourselves in each other. Can people make a lasting bond from being flung together so in fear? It seemed we did, and that at last, still struggling in each other's arms, we fell into a kind of sleep. And when, after a long time, it grew light, there was a sort of quiet over the city. The smoke and the stench remained, but there were no more gigantic clashes, no crowds fleeing and pursuing, only a silent and terrible tiredness.

They came, of course, and dragged us out, and I was terrified again, but in the midst of terror found a minute to remember and smile at my poor mother and her lost hope for me to be a Trojan matron like herself. No matron I would ever be nor wish to be, but prayed just to stay close all my days to my new sister, Helen. And that prayer was answered. I did stay near her, but she was a queen then and with no time to spend thinking about a prisoner-slave, part of the spoils of Troy.

Once more, tonight, there were screams and running feet and voices raising the alarm and quiet at last and many hands pulling us from our place of refuge, but this time they were more gentle than before by far. Her servants stopped the blaze and quenched that sheet of flame and led her off, pressing their hands to her temple and supporting her and soothing her with balms and cloths dampened with oil and water. And I, not important enough to merit concern, lucky even to escape blame for the accident, stumbled to my pallet in the alcove. I felt, and still feel, very ill, but I have been much acquainted with fear and violence, and I know it does strange things to the body and the mind. My hearing has gone, and I can no longer see properly the things about me. I have lain for a long time, seared by the flames ignited by her carelessness and fanned by her indifference. But since the hoard of memories has become unlocked, I rehearse again the things that happened from the moment that the Trojans saw the wooden stallion left by the Greeks upon the strand.

The horse was drawn up on the beach, and the people stood goggling at it, not speaking, their cheeks bulging with food, nudging and laughing at each other. Then Laocoön, blazing mad, rushed down from the temple crying, "You blithering idiots, leave that thing alone. Have you taken leave of the little mother wit you have? Do you think the Greeks have suddenly had an attack of homesickness and gone rushing off for a bit of home cooking? Don't you know Ulysses better than that? Why, they are most to be feared when they come laden with geegaws."

The people grew sullen at this, and one from the crowd said, "It was you, Laocoön, who said the Greeks were men like ourselves."

"Yes, Laocoön," the others took up the chorus jeeringly, "we all speak the same language you said."

A murmur of resentment rose like smoke above the angry crowd. My father grew so furious that he raised his spear and hurled it at the painted horse's belly. When it hit, it made the horse ring with an almost human sound — "Ooh-Ow" — and the crowd for a moment recoiled, struck by uncertainty, wavering between their natural truculence and fear. Only for a second did they pause, though. The noise soon rose again; the crowd milled round the horse, stroking its flanks and offering their half-baked opinions in place of wisdom. The prisoner that the Greeks had left behind spoke his piece, and everyone began to shout and argue. And in the midst of all this pandemonium two giant serpents left the sea and slithered across the sand, swiftly and deadly, aligned like horses yoked together before a chariot.

First they seized the twins, Demetrius and Alex, and my father rushed to their aid, hacking vainly at the coiling monsters while the crowd looked on, unmoving and disinclined to stir themselves to help. Then, having wrought their deadly purpose on the boys until they fell, two lifeless bodies on the strand, the great beasts turned their sinuous mass upon Laocoön, my father. And there on the beach he fought his last battle while his neighbors stood and stared. No one raised a hand to hurl a stone or shout; all merely stood there, gaping like an audience at some circus or public execution watching a slave or common criminal mauled by a bear.

So this one clear voice of reason so often raised in protest against the coils and feeble arguments of the common herd was quenched at last. He fell, caught in the tentacles of these mindless venomous serpents, and not a single Trojan raised a hand in his defense. And thus my father died. Perhaps, now that I remember, I shall not need to dream of him again.

Conversation Pieces

Lilian and Henry Sparrow, ever since their daughter Elspeth had married a GI, had taken a proprietary interest in the entire North American continent. They were self-appointed ambassadors, authorities, and defenders of the state. Their information about the place, gleaned from their son-in-law before he returned stateside, and fed subsequently by their daughter's letters, stood to gain considerably from the visit of their newly acquired American relatives, the parents of their son-in-law, Marvin.

It was the nearest they ever hoped to get to firsthand knowledge of America. The Sparrows always went to a nearby seaside resort for their annual holiday, the most extensive preparation for which was the sewing of pockets in all her husband's underwear by Lilian Sparrow. These, when secured at the top with safety pins, provided ample protection against the purse-snatchers and pickpockets of which she had inordinate terror. Because of this terror, any form of travel that prevented her from holding in her lap the smaller items of luggage and keeping the larger ones under her feet was unthinkable. Travel abroad for the Sparrows was completely out of the question.

But Mrs. Sparrow had an additional reason for anticipating very eagerly the arrival of her new American connections. She had a strong competitive streak in her makeup, and it had been her overriding ambition to see that her daughter not only married well but married better than any of the local girls. She had dreamed of a doctor, a dentist, or a vicar, and had come near to despair when Elspeth showed no signs of sharing her mother's ambitions and had selected her boyfriends on the unreliable grounds of appearance and personality. Lilian had wondered at times if the girl had her head screwed on the right way at all. She had, however, taken a new lease on life when Elspeth started working as a secretary at the nearby American Air Force base. In Lilian Sparrow's view an American son-in-law quite equaled a well-educated one, such a match bespeaking as it did a life of affluence and luxury.

The emigration of her only daughter was easily offset by the prestige to be reaped from the marriage. She envisaged streams of letters bearing the ammunition for beating out rival mothers in terms of large cars, big houses, fine clothes. And indeed her hopes had been realized when Elspeth brought home Marvin Zack and introduced him as her intended. The neighbors could laugh all they liked at his crew cut, his accent, and his cheap-looking clothes (khaki pants, army jacket, tennis shoes), but it was clear from his car and from the size of the solitaire diamond he gave Elspeth that he was better off by far than any of the village lads.

It was true that in the months after her daughter had left home, Lilian wished there were more visible signs of this good marriage to display to the community. She tired of boasting about how well Elspeth was doing and flashing photographs around to prove it. For this reason, she hailed the visit of the senior Zacks as a face-saving and prestige-creating event. It was particularly gratifying to her to learn that the Zacks were traveling in the most ostentatious style. They planned to rent a car at the airport, stay overnight at the Midland Hotel in Manchester, and then come on to the Sparrows for five days before proceeding south to London and the Continent. "Seems like money's no object with them," said Lilian Sparrow in the greengrocer's shop. Five days did seem rather a large slice from the Zacks' crowded itinerary, but the Zacks, like the Sparrows, had their own reasons for attaching importance to meeting their new English relatives and tarrying so long with them.

At the root of their eagerness was their rampant sociability. Bea Zack, in particular, filled her calendar to the saturation point with coffee parties, luncheon parties, card parties, cocktail parties, dinner parties, open houses, potluck suppers, picnics, and excursions. At the hint of an engagement, wedding, or pregnancy she was first off the mark with a shower. As soon as Thanksgiving was over, she was planning Christmas festivities, New Year's Eve bashes, and right on through to Valentine's Day, when she traditionally had a come-and-go supper for all the married couples in her church circle. Charles Zack's energy was slightly less than his wife's, but he panted along close behind her, telling himself that it was good for business. (He was in real estate.) And so, although both Zacks habitually surveyed their wall calendar with mock horror and professed to yearn for an evening at home or a free weekend, they counted the hours spent at home alone as so much wasted time and wouldn't have known what to do with them if they had any.

The main snag in all this hypersocial activity with little time for rumination between parties was that it was hard to find conversational material to sustain the frequent gatherings that often featured the same cast of characters. Consequently, all experiences outside the social round tended to be relegated to a peripheral level with the sole purpose of feeding and providing subjects of interest for the main forum. And it so happened that the marriage of Marvin to a darling little girl from England had been a boon in this situation. It yielded just the right kind of yarns, jokes, and sentimental personal anecdotes (the last were particularly popular with the women). It also supplied a wealth of props and audiovisual aids to be passed around and read aloud at social functions. These included extracts from letters, photographs, and recipes for such exotic items as plum pudding, treacle toffee, mint sauce, and lemon curd. Bea hoped to gather much more material when she met in person her English counterpart, Lilian Sparrow.

The two couples, therefore, with their mutual dependence and their common lack of consuming interests, had the basis for a sound and lasting relationship. Of course, there were bound to be differences between them, some of a personal and some of a cultural nature. A casual observer had only to see Bea and Lilian standing side by side, to be struck by their utter incongruity.

Bea Zack was one of those wiry, energetic women without an ounce of fat on her spare frame or any possibility of gaining any. In many cultures she would have been considered ugly, but the fashion of the day was in her favor, as long as she avoided shorts and bathing suits. She was slender and youthful, and jauntily flung her bird-thin legs across each other when she sat down. Flat-chested, she looked her best in long-sleeved, high-necked wool dresses that hugged her undernourished frame and in suits with the pencil-slim skirts that were the fashion of the time.

These were also the days of bouffant hairdos, and the great puff of hair was quite flattering to Mrs. Zack's small, rather pinched face and wrinkly skin. On top of her coiffure she wore velvet bows (of which she had a great many, in colors that matched all her outfits) and various kinds of net and lace toppings. Mrs. Sparrow, who thought that otherwise Mrs. Zack was as elegant as a duchess, looked askance at these fripperies, because if there was one item which she considered indispensable to female dignity, it was a hat. Only the poorest of poor women in the town, the ones that worked in the mills or on the pit crew, went about in scarves, shawls, or woolen pixie hoods. No one went bareheaded. In fact, Mrs. Sparrow had been quite unsettled by seeing on a television newsreel some pictures of the Queen and Princess Margaret wearing scarves at the Badminton horse trials. She thought that the Queen Mother, who was her ideal, would never have appeared in public so unsuitably dressed.

She, Mrs. Sparrow, had a whole rack of hats wrapped in cellophane in the top of the wardrobe in her bedroom. Any one of them would have done service in a fancy dress parade, with an excellent chance of winning first prize in the "most humorous headdress" category. For winter she had the fur headpieces of Nubian slaves; for summer she had wicker headgear that resembled inverted chamberpots or coal scuttles; for everyday, year-round wear she had a whole line of turbans in jersey and wool and linen, all reminiscent of the last days of the British raj; and for vicarage garden parties and weddings she had wide-brimmed, blossom-dripping hats in which a cowboy might have emerged from a shootout in a flower shop.

In her younger days Mrs. Sparrow had been as slender as Bea Zack, but it had been her misfortune to live in a time and a region where slender was synonymous with skinny and where the word used to praise female beauty was "bonny," suggesting a second or third generation reared in such comfortable circumstances that there was always enough to eat. Perhaps it was for this reason that Lilian Sparrow had not fought the burgeoning of her figure. It had now reached the point where her bust was a big single unit, like a bolster wrapped around her chest. Her waistline had disappeared altogether, and she had a natural bustle behind which lifted the hems of her dresses to a dangerously high level. If she thought of her shape at all, she would have used the word "motherly" rather than "stout" and deemed it an entirely appropriate and inevitable condition for a woman of her age. In fact, she had not thought of her shape at all until she clapped eyes on Bea Zack and heard Henry say that she didn't look at all like a woman in her fifties.

Happily, Lilian Sparrow had very little personal vanity. It was perhaps the one area in which she was not quick to take offense. Henry could tease her all he wished about her heft, and she was the first to laugh. And so the fact that she looked exactly twice as old and three times as wide as Bea Zack gave her not a moment's pause. All went swimmingly between the two couples from the beginning. In the first hours of their meeting the Zacks said "when you come over to stay with us" so often that such a visit moved into the realm of probability. When Mrs. Sparrow mentioned the frequent reports of lost luggage and stolen money on long journeys, Charles Zack waived away the objection.

"Get traveler's checks. Take out plenty of insurance and forget about the luggage," he said. (Insurance was a sideline of his business.)

There was not even any initial shyness, which was strange because Lilian Sparrow tended to be very standoffish with strangers. But even she was completely disarmed by Bea Zack's warmth and unbridled enthusiasm for everything. Bea wanted to experience every facet of the English Way of Life while she was over there—tea with milk, English breakfast, even a hot-water bottle in her bed. When she spotted the teapot carried in under its little knitted ski-bonnet, she said it was the cutest thing she'd ever seen in her whole life. Lilian Sparrow immediately presented her with one she had just finished knitting for a bring-and-buy sale, and Bea said she couldn't wait to put it on her own coffeepot and serve coffee to her sewing circle. It would be a perfect conversation piece. She applied this designation to many of the objects she acquired in the next day or two, prompt-

ing Henry Sparrow to think she was the last person in the world to
need such props. But no one took offense or said anything out of the
way. Lilian Sparrow, who winced the first time they called her "Lil",
soon got used to the name, although she had more difficulty in bringing herself to come out and call Charles Zack "Chuck", as he insisted
she do. She managed "Er-Chuck" when it was absolutely necessary
but usually avoided calling him anything at all.

On the first evening, after the meal was over and cleared away
(Bea had insisted on helping with the dishes, and Lilian had rather
dubiously provided her with a frilly apron intended as a gift rather
than for practical use), both couples settled down to look at each
other's collections of photographs.

It was a somewhat uneven exchange because the Sparrows' contribution consisted of a series of scrapbooks with a haphazard assortment of snapshots and newspaper clippings, none of the photographs taken by the Sparrows themselves but all of them somewhat
clumsily glued into the album by Lilian Sparrow. There were pictures
of Elspeth as a child, in stiff studio poses, looking unhappy. There
were school snaps and group photographs and later ones taken by
promenade photographers on seaside holidays. Others were group
photographs taken by relatives who had acquired box cameras but
never quite mastered them. These tended to be black-and-white pictures (either over- or underexposed) of a huge expanse of sky with
the people huddled in one corner, scowling as if facing a firing
squad.

The Zacks, on the other hand, had a box of 35 millimeter slides
which they inserted into a viewing device so that the Sparrows, peering inside, were treated to three-dimensional dioramas in glorious
technicolor of a series of gala social occasions. (It was, in fact, with
such glimpses of a life of glamor and color and fun that Marvin Zack
had wooed and finally seduced Elspeth Sparrow.) The viewing went
slowly because it required a great deal of commentary, which Bea
Zack provided in exact detail. The phrase "when you come over"
crept in again very frequently amid the explanations, some of which
were technical and some merely descriptive. Bea regaled the Sparrows with an account of the surprise party which friends had given
for their twentieth wedding anniversary. She gave a long rigmarole

about how they had been lured from home, entertained, and brought back home to find their house and garden beseiged by friends wishing them a happy anniversary. Lilian Sparrow, goggling at the groups of men roaring with laughter, wearing open-necked shirts in primary colors, and waving beer cans, shuddered at the thought of having such an army invade the house in her absence. Suppose they saw the old threadbare towels she used for everyday? Suppose it was washing day, and there were racks of clothes drying all over the place? But then she had noticed that the diurnal round of domestic duties which controlled her life seemed to have no place at all in Bea Zack's. There were many such details which puzzled her. The American Way of Life, instead of becoming more understandable through the presence of the Zacks, was being rendered more and more incomprehensible. Mrs. Sparrow, like all her neighbors, always did her washing on Monday, her ironing on Tuesday, and so on. She intended to ask Bea at some later date when she did hers and how she coped on bad drying days.

By the time they had gone through the entire pile of the Zacks' slides, Mrs. Sparrow was more confused than ever and had a great many questions that she didn't quite know how to ask. She had seen pictures of Marvin at his first formal, with the girl he was dating at that time. She was a real doll and a cheerleader, but with plenty on the ball. (Bea explained the technicalities as they went along.) They had seen indoor parties with all the women in long dresses. (The men for some reason didn't seem to match the formality of the occasion and were still wearing colored shirts and no ties.) They had seen Christmas parties with poinsettias and huge, ceiling-high Christmas trees, all sparkling with baubles and lights and banked high underneath with bright-colored packages.

Chuck interrupted Bea at this point to say that Christmas around their place was always like a three-ring circus. Lilian, searching for an appropriate response, said it was here too, what with the church choir coming round to sing carols and so on. She said that for her part she was always glad (this was true) when it was over.

They saw outdoor scenes with wonderful white snow in winter, and everyone wrapped up in scarves and boots. They saw marvelous summer scenes with weinie roasts and outdoor barbeques. At these the men in aprons were cooking things over outdoor grills, waving in one hand the ubiquitous beer can and holding in the other special prongs for turning and poking the food.

Bea was a great one for gadgets said Chuck, the provider of gadgets, with affectionate pride. Bea said she had nothing on him and he hadn't looked back since she gave him a barbeque for Father's Day. He cooked outdoors all summer long and was the expert in the family at cooking steaks and hamburgers. (Here she winked in sly complicity at Lilian.)

"When you stay with us . . . ," said Chuck for the umpteenth time, though Lilian Sparrow wasn't sure that she fancied a hamburger cooked on one of those things.

Then back they went to scenes of more merriment. Again and again there were the surprise parties. Bea never tired of explaining the circumstances of the surprises. The Zacks were invariably caught unawares in the most comical circumstances and appeared at the parties underdressed or overdressed as if for church. As Bea recalled these times, Chuck laughed until the tears ran down his face. The Sparrows, not wanting to appear killjoys, laughed along, though Henry could not for the life of him see how they could have been taken by surprise with such regularity, and Lilian thought she would have approached any festive occasion with acute anxiety.

"I just love parties," said Bea Zack redundantly. Lilian Sparrow said she did too but there was very little time for them, what with her church work on top of all the housework and shopping, and anyway she rather liked a quiet life. Crowds tended to bring on one of her migraines.

"You and me both," cried Chuck Zack. "Give me a baseball game on the TV and I'm set for the evening, but Bea here won't even let me watch the World Series unless I see it at someone else's place."

"Don't believe him," said Bea. "Just try leaving him behind when you go out some place."

"I don't trust her on her own," whispered Chuck loudly to Lilian, pretending to impart a secret. "She's always the best-looking gal in the crowd."

Bea screeched at this, and Lilian felt obliged to laugh too, although she thought the remark was in very questionable taste. She disliked any open display of affection between people and had noted the disconcerting tendency of the guests in some of the pictures to link arms or even throw their arms around each other's necks in ostentatious displays of friendship. She hoped that when she visited, the Americans would not take such liberties with her.

As the days passed, it was this uncurbed gregariousness in the Zacks which most puzzled the Sparrows. Bea Zack went in and out of the house and up and down the road, halloing to anyone she saw for the second time and waving to them for all the world, thought Lilian Sparrow, like the Queen Mum touring the London slums. Her friendliness was galling to the Sparrows for two reasons. In the first place, entrenched as they were in their position as intermediaries and interpreters, they had had no intention of allowing direct contact between the foreigners and their neighbors. They had forseen no contact whatsoever and had expected, after the visit, to give out bits of suitable information gradually like official communiqués.

In the second place, the Sparrows believed in keeping the neighbors at a distance. They had not liked the look of the people on one side the minute they had moved into their house. Consequently, they had never exchanged a word with them until Bea Zack started raving about their herbaceous border and asking the names of some perfectly ordinary perennials that anyone in his right mind could see were stunted for want of manure.

With the family on the other side, matters were even more embarrassing. The Sparrows had at one time been friendly with the Braddocks, but they had had a falling-out five years ago and subsequently had not been on speaking terms. Mrs. Sparrow considered them not quite the thing. Their daughter had made an improvident marriage to a traveling salesman, a shiftless, fly-by-night person no one knew anything about. To make matters worse, the girl had discovered her mistake, left her husband, and returned home with a child. Mrs. Sparrow felt that this situation lowered the tone of the whole neighborhood. Her irritation knew no bounds when Bea Zack spotted the little lad playing in the garden, pronounced him "cute as a button" (which he wasn't), addressed him as "honey", and threatened to kidnap him and take him right back with her to Kokomo, Indiana. As Lilian Sparrow said later to Henry, "You sometimes

wonder if she's all there, the way she carries on." She tried to talk
some sense into her guest by informing her that the Braddocks were
not their kind, but Bea just looked at her with incomprehension.

Lilian Sparrow had even more cause for wonderment the next day
when she introduced Bea to the butcher and his wife. (The need to
butter up the tradespeople was back of this particular concession.)
When asked how she liked England, Bea Zack said "just fine" and
went on quite gratuitously to tell the entire shop (there was a queue
of women right out the door and down the street, all with their ears
cocked) that she had been scraping and saving for this trip for years.
No doubt she was self-conscious about the large car at the curb and
wanted to reassure the grocery-laden housewives that she was just
plain folks like them. Mrs. Sparrow nearly dropped through the saw-
dust-covered floor at this breach of etiquette, for "swanking" was a
time-honored local custom. Anyone who could afford a car, a fur
coat, or any of the more conspicuous consumables would have died
rather than admit they scrounged and saved for them. They were expected to act as if they teethed on silver spoons and bought such
items all the time, no matter that the entire town was speculating on
the source (came up on the football pools? cashed in on an insurance
policy?) and making dire predictions about the consequences of such
profligacy (end up in the workhouse if they don't watch out, seen
folks before like that and when they die they don't leave enough for a
decent funeral). So Mrs. Sparrow had every right to be shocked. She
lost no time in taking Bea aside and warning her, "It doesn't do to let
folk know all your business." She began to suspect quite seriously at
this point that Bea Zack had a bit of something missing.

Exactly the same kind of thing happened when they all went out to
Blackpool. Mrs. Sparrow had thoroughly enjoyed riding in the big
car and was delighted when the Zacks insisted on taking them for
lunch to the Clifton Hotel, right on the sea front, which the Sparrows had previously seen only from the outside. It was very formal,
with white linen on the tables and waiters in black ties with serviettes
over one arm. Lilian Sparrow settled into her chair, torn between
thoughts of swanking about the occasion in the future and trying not
to look too impressed in the present. But she was shaken out of her
conflict by Bea Zack, who knew no better than to start chatting to

the waiter as if he were her equal. Lilian Sparrow thought everyone knew that you were supposed to treat members of the servile occupations with lofty disdain-verging-on-contempt. They expected it and would respond to anything less with their own kind of contempt. And here was Bea Zack making up to the young man in the most undignified way, saying he reminded her of a certain actor in an English comedy she'd seen on televison. She appealed to Lilian to help her out with the name. Lilian stared stonily at the menu, but this carrying-on put her off her food, and she told Henry later that she couldn't say she enjoyed the meal at all.

Before it was over, Bea Zack had wormed out of the young man that he was saving up for a trip round the world and had caused Lilian a choking fit by telling him that her son Marvin had worked as a waiter during his summers in high school. She also wrote her address down for him so that he could look her up if he was ever anywhere near Kokomo on his tour round the world. Lilian Sparrow had no doubt whatsoever that their party was the laughingstock of the hotel, even if the waiter did accompany them to the door, dancing attendance on Bea the whole time. Lilian herself was a stingy tipper and rationalized by saying that overtipping was the height of vulgarity. It made her blazing to note the overly large tip Chuck Zack left on the table. (There was no mistaking the crackling bill, and Lilian Sparrow thought she would rather give to the church than throw it away on people who were likely to spend it on drink.)

By the end of the third day Lilian Sparrow began to feel that the whole situation was hopelessly out of control. Bea Zack had somehow managed to make inroads into several houses on Surrenden Drive, and Lilian Sparrow hardly dared think of the indiscreet confidences, the addresses traded, and the promises of Christmas cards.

"I shall sure hate to leave this little ole town and all the friends we've made here," said Bea.

"That's Bea for you," said Chuck. "Makes friends everywhere she goes. She should have been an ambassador."

"No one can tell me the English aren't friendly," said Bea. "Friendliest people in the world once you get to know them."

Mrs. Sparrow thought with dismay of all the damage done in the last few days and how it might take years to repair it and restore the neighbors to their proper distance again. If that Mrs. Braddock thought she would be shouting over the fence "Had a Christmas card from America," she had another think coming. Once the Zacks left, Lilian Sparrow intended to cut her dead if she met her on the street.

Nevertheless, for all her resolve, the strain was beginning to tell on Mrs. Sparrow. Her nerves, which at the best of times were likely to play her up, were showing signs of wear and tear. The worry of not knowing what Bea Zack was going to do next, the pressure of getting meals on the table and being constantly on the go had made her irritable and on edge. Had it not been so, the visit might have gone off without a hitch. On the other hand, perhaps the relationship was doomed from the start.

The storm blew up quite without warning on the evening of the third day. Like a seastorm it flared up out of an unusual quietude. They had had their evening meal and were sitting around the fire in the lounge. They had exhausted all the photographs and all the slides and all the possible topics of conversation. Even Bea Zack's constant chatter seemed temporarily to have run down. Lilian Sparrow looked at the clock on the mantelpiece and thought that in half an hour she would put on the kettle for the cup of tea and piece of cake she liked to have before going to bed. She sighed and said, "I often wonder at this time of day what our Elspeth's doing."

"I wonder what she does all the time," said Bea Zack ambiguously, "with that dinky house and that dinky garden, not that she takes much interest in either one."

Accustomed as she was by now to the shock value of Bea's remarks, Lilian Sparrow was taken by surprise at this sally.

"Well, what should she do?" she asked in genuine curiosity.

"I think she should get herself a job," replied Bea Zack firmly.

"A job?" said Lilian Sparrow, as if she had overheard an obscenity. "A job? You don't get married to get a job!" She always spoke of women working as if it were the highest form of indecency.

"I don't see why not," said Bea Zack. "I always go in and help Chuck at busy times or if one of the girls calls in sick."

"Sure," said Chuck, perhaps sensing that something was going wrong. "Bea enjoys it, enjoys meeting the folks. Elly could find something part-time if she wanted to. That way they'd get the house and the car paid off sooner."

"The house and the car paid off?" said Lilian Sparrow incredulously. "You don't mean to tell me they bought that car on the never-never?" This was the first time she had heard any details of her daughter's financial arrangements, and it shocked her to the core. She had assumed that the junior Zacks were managing more or less the way she did when she and Henry were married thirty years before. Henry had saved up for seven years, and her own father had helped them buy the house. In her experience only shiftless and irresponsible people bought things before they could pay for them, or got married before they could afford to.

"How else they gonna buy a car?" asked Chuck Zack in wonder. "The GI bill only pays for Marv's schooling, you know."

"If Elly helped out a bit, he could keep right on in school till he gets his degree," added Bea Zack.

"Keep on *in school?*" Lilian Sparrow almost screamed. "Keep on in school! Why, he's a married man with a wife to support. Has he no sense of responsibility? What business does he have going to school in the first place?"

Mrs. Sparrow was so blazing she felt a migraine coming on as sure as anything, but she was so riled up nothing could prevent her from coming right out and saying what was on her mind.

"I don't know how you do things where you come from," she said, "but they certainly aren't the way we do them. We don't buy things we can't afford. Why when we got married, our parents helped us with the house, and we got things gradually as we needed them. We saved up seven years before we got married and waited another five to have Elspeth. I don't believe in women working either. We never had a babysitter the whole time she was growing up. That's not what you get married for. And going to school! Just plain irresponsible. No sense of responsiblity. She'd have been better off staying here. And her name's Elspeth. I don't know why you keep calling her Elly. I never heard anything so . . . so *common.*"

The last word seemed to bubble up of its own accord, but once it was spoken the force of it hit Mrs. Sparrow like a personal revelation. She knew that was the word that had simmered at the back of her mind all week long, although she had not articulated it until this moment. Downright common, that was what the Zacks were. Bea with her loud laugh and familiar ways and her little cheap nets and ribbons in place of proper hats. And working part-time. And goodness knows what else. Mrs. Sparrow was beginning at last to understand these people. It had taken her a while because they were foreigners, but now she had wrestled them into a familiar slot. And she knew at last what Elspeth's life must be like and what manner of character Marvin Zack was. He was downright shiftless, just like the salesman that Betty Braddock next door had run off with. But because he was American, she, Lilian Sparrow, had not been able to see him for what he really was. She felt that she had been the victim of a confidence man or trickster of some kind. It made her blazing to think she had been so taken in and duped. And then the gall of his parents coming over and lording it over the entire neighborhood like Lord and Lady Docker in that big car, while she, Lilian Sparrow, waited on them hand and foot, trailing after them and cooking meals. Well, they had had the last cup of tea they were going to have in this house. And with a toss of her head she got up, left the room, banged the door, and went off to bed without pausing to fill a hot-water bottle. She did not, of course, fall asleep. How could she, aggravated as she was by the thought of the Zacks under the same roof. She thought bitterly that if they'd been English she wouldn't have had them in the house, let alone eating and sleeping in the best bedroom for three nights. For hours she didn't get a wink of sleep, though Henry beside her slept soundly, just as he had throughout the air raids.

In the next bedroom the Zacks weren't sleeping all that well either. Oh, Chuck finally dropped off. Bea always said he'd get a night's sleep even if a tornado ripped the roof right off the house. But she lay awake, looking about her in the light of the street lamps that shone through the cracks in the badly fitting curtains. She surveyed the room with contempt. It was an ugly, dark room, full of heavy, old-fashioned furniture that she would have thrown out long ago, though her antique-collecting friends might find some use for it – the great wardrobe, the tallboy with claw feet, the single light dangling from the ceiling in a cheap lampshade. Everything ramshackle and mismatched. Just typical of the people and the place. No proper method of lighting and heating. Electric heaters plugged in all over the house. Not enough hot water for a decent bath. No shower. And those Sparrows, cheerfully plodding along from one cup of tea to the next, thinking they were offering a treat if they gave you a slice of cake with it. She remembered her daughter-in-law Elly, who refused to work or help out or do anything except read a book a day from the public library. Just typical. Lackadaisical, no get-up-and-go, no ambition, no enterprise, and no fun on top of it all. Just a dull, half-dead, joyless existence. And to think, thought Bea Zack, almost dissolving into tears, that we sent our boys over here to fight for people like this. Young, promising boys and many of them lost their lives and limbs. Toward dawn she fell into a fitful sleep, and when she woke up she was exhausted. She thought she'd give anything for a cup of coffee and wondered how soon they could get one if they headed straight back to Manchester. She thought she'd throw up if she had to down another cup of milky tea or face another bite of cold, rubbery toast.

Mrs. Sparrow finally fell asleep too, but she had a dreadful nightmare. She dreamed that she dashed out for a loaf and when she got back, she found the house full of neighbors shouting "Surprise! Surprise!" Bea Zack had malevolently organized a party in her absence and invited the neighbors to pry into every corner of the house. It was washing day, and their underwear was draped about the kitchen and other rooms. There were her old corsets that she wore for everyday, Henry's combinations with the stains in the crotch, his old pajamas that she had meant to replace but kept patching and making last a bit longer. When she woke up she was feverish and soaking with sweat, and her head was pounding with one of the worst migraines she had had in years.

There was no question of her getting out of bed, and Henry Sparrow thought he might have to go next-door-but-one and call the doctor. The Zacks were very understanding and said they would just leave a day earlier. They quietly loaded their suitcases into the back of the car and drove off without breakfast and without waving to any of the neighbors, some of whom were opening their front doors and picking up the milk bottles from the doorsteps. They barely even said good-bye to Henry Sparrow and just said they hoped Lilian would soon be back on her feet.

Lilian, in fact, was on her feet the minute she heard the front door close, and from behind her bedroom curtain she watched them drive off down the street. Then she got back into bed, heaved a great sigh, and fell asleep. It was afternoon before she woke up and teatime before she ventured tentatively downstairs, as if there might be some lingering contamination.

Henry made the tea, and they sat by the fire drinking it and toasting tea cakes on the glowing coals. Lilian was in her old worn dressing gown and carpet slippers with slashes cut in them to accommodate her bunions. She felt relaxed for the first time in days.

"I couldn't have stood another minute of it," she said. "I couldn't *abide* that woman. I never want to see her again, and I wouldn't go over there if you paid me a million pounds." Henry Sparrow agreed that a visit was no longer feasible. (He'd had his doubts all along.)

"People like that make me sick," said Lilian Sparrow. "All outside show. All talk! I bet they haven't a penny behind them if you care to go into it. Nothing in the bank and buying everything on the HP — big cars, big holidays, big parties. Well none of it fooled me. And she works, that's the top and bottom of it. It came out at long last. 'I go in when Chuck needs me' Ha! that didn't fool me. I bet she's doing a nine-to-five job, that's how she keeps so skinny, running about to work every day. No wonder she needs her own car. And has to have him doing the cooking! Did you notice how thin her neck was? Scrawny! I bet they keep a poor table into the bargain. Grilling hamburgers on that outdoor thing! I bet they never see a proper piece of meat. Hamburgers and hot dogs! Well, you wouldn't get me eating hamburgers and hot dogs whatever you grilled them on. I never have been able to stand rissoles." Henry Sparrow agreed with her, but said that Elspeth was the one he felt sorry for.

"Well, I do too," said Lilian Sparrow, "but you can't say she didn't get herself into this. She never did have an ounce of sense when it came to boys. Always thinking of having a good time instead of using her head. I tell you one thing," she said. "At least if she's got a worthless man, no one around this town will know about it. We shan't make fools of ourselves like that lot next door."

"And it's a good thing too," said Henry Sparrow, "that we never told anyone we might be going to America."

"Well," said Lilian Sparrow, "I've always said it's best if you don't let anyone know your business. And the less you have to do with your neighbors, the better. My mother always said that."

When she finally got around to clearing out the best bedroom, she was surprised to find that Bea Zack had left behind the tea cosy, the toast rack she intended to use for letters, the union-jack tea caddy, the hot-water bottle in its novelty case, and all the other items she had eagerly latched on to as conversation pieces. Since they were sitting right in the middle of the eiderdown, Mrs. Sparrow couldn't help feeling that the failure to take them along was deliberate.

The Celebrant

Enid Brocklebank never stopped being astonished that wherever in the world she was — in her home, in the terra incognita of a strange hotel room, even in the arms of a loved one — on a certain day in the late fall she woke knowing with instant and complete clarity *today is the birthday of Karen Green.*

In spite of her neglect of every kind of family observance and anniversary, national holiday, or religious festival, she never failed in some way to celebrate and sanctify this one day of the year. She woke always, as she had long ago in her narrow childhood bed, telling herself without hesitation that on this day in some distant part of the globe (if she were still alive) Karen Green (if that were still her name) would be having another birthday and being wished many happy returns.

But of course at that earlier time, it was not Karen Green or her birthday that Enid was chiefly thinking of. That event was merely the vehicle or code or cloak for another thought more rare and wonderful. What she really thought was *today I shall see my Cousin Angela* or, more exactly, *today I shall be IN THE PRESENCE OF my Cousin Angela,* for her being shed itself in that little world like the aura of monarchy or saintliness.

It was this thought alone that tempered the dread with which Enid looked forward to birthday parties, these affairs being planned by the parents according to their perennial misunderstanding of the children's pleasures. The chief purpose of the parties, in fact, since this all took place during a time of war, was to preserve the illusion that the children were having, in her father's often-used phrase, *some semblance of a normal childhood*. The parents lived under the threat of doom — famine, blitz, enemy occupation, deportation, and death — and it was in this context that for their reassurance they organized birthday parties. So the village children received invitations, accepted them, got spruced up and marched off to parties far more often than would have been their fate had they lived in a time of peace.

Enid's Cousin Angela was not actually a native of the village, but was a frequent visitor from the adjacent town where she lived. The two girls were often thrown together because their mother-sisters found it convenient to have them amuse each other while they, the mothers, indulged their secret vices of smoking woodbine cigarettes, drinking strong tea, and gossiping. Moreover, Angela, because of her stateliness and gravity, was deemed a good influence, and she and Enid spent many weekends keeping out of mischief together (the parents' idea of mischief running to torn clothes, shattered china ornaments, and devastated flower beds, all forms of desecration likely to ensue if Enid were allowed to play with the village lads rather than with her Cousin Angela).

But it was not the fact that the three of them came from separate villages which made it surprising that Enid or Angela should have been invited to Karen Green's birthday party, it was something less easy to define. There clung to the family of Karen Green the effluvium of scandal which could be traced back to the youth of her grandmother. It was precisely this: when the grandmother had married, it was *because she had to*. The children were not aware of this fact, but they sensed very clearly that some kind of contamination had permeated the entire Green clan. It was a taint that they all carried, whether they were born into the family or married into it, and it affected everything they did. The grandmother was florid, boisterous, and obviously unrepentant for the lapses of her youth. She also had a seedy occupation as a "corseteer," which meant that the women of the village went to her house and disappeared into an upstairs bedroom to try on corsets, buy them, and leave the house with discreet but shameful brown packages under their arms. Moreover, in her spare time the grandmother made hooked rugs, blending and braiding an assortment of clothing, including undergarments, which normally the villagers forbore to hang out on their washing lines, let alone shamelessly weave into doormats and hearth rugs. Perhaps in defiance of this dishonorable lineage (or in some other way connected with it), all the Greens had an air of sexual disreputability. The mother of Karen Green had a way of hitching up her skirts when she sat down that was embarrassing to men and women alike. She was said to be oversexed, and Enid's mother said of her with a sniff: "Not very lady-like."

In later years Enid came to see that the place was a quintessentially pure English village, unchanged since its beginning and peopled by archetypal English characters. When she read Chaucer, she met them there, every one, and she recognized instantly in Alysoun, the Wife of Bath, the direct ancestor of her next-door neighbor, the grandmother of Karen Green.

In view of her ignominious connections it was beyond Enid's comprehension that one day, long after the birthday party and the war were over, Karen Green should have turned to her quite casually during a chance meeting in the street and said, "You know, your Cousin Angela was quite *disgusting*" (she pronounced it "dis-CUST-ing"). Karen Green made remarks that resonated down endless corridors of time and memory. Enid could still remember that when she came to ask her to the birthday party and to explain that they would see her home afterward, she added, as if it were entirely inconsequential, "Oh, and we've invited your Cousin Angela as well."

Enid was as much astonished as excited, for Angela had her own kind of, not stigma exactly, but apartness. Her mother had married in a way that was certainly not disreputable, but unusual. Of the two sisters, Enid's mother had been the plain one and Angela's mother the beauty. (*"And you can see where that gets you,"* said Enid's mother, though the meaning of that remark was lost on Enid.) On account of her beauty and grace, Angela's mother had become a skilled ballroom dancer and had married a man nobody knew, a man she had met in a ballroom-dancing competition in Blackpool. While it was true that most Italian immigrants were of marginal respectability and did fly-by-night jobs, like peddling ice cream, this was not true of Angela's father. He was a member of an established family which had for years run a prosperous bakery in a neighboring market town. When Enid accompanied Angela to her church, she saw a large plaque on the wall: BLESSED BE THE ESTATES OF FRANCIS VITALE. This was the name of Angela's grandfather and of her father and of her little brother, although everyone called him Johnny. The marriage, then, as Enid's mother said, was not so bad and yet not so good either. Enid's father said, "Francis isn't a bad chap, if only he wouldn't dress like a bookie." So there it was. Once Karen Green said to Angela, "You're a Roman Catholic, aren't you?" in the insinuating tone that one might use to say "Your dad's a conchy, isn't he?" But Angela replied very simply and without emphasis, "Yes, I am a Catholic," and Karen Green for once in her cheeky life was at a loss for words. It was entirely typical of Angela to remain inviolate and imperturbable, as if someone had drawn a circle around where she stood and forbidden anyone to step inside. She maintained her perfect distance and stateliness and dignity.

Enid knew, therefore, that amid all the confusion of the party — Karen Green flinging open the door and grabbing her present before anyone had time even to lift the knocker, the mismatched throng of babbling children, the bossy grown-ups — there would be Angela, standing in her almost tangible circle of radiance and beauty, and she would look up and say, "Hello Eeny." And Enid would say, a little breathlessly, "Oh hello, Angela," for no one ever dreamed of giving Angela the kind of nickname that stuck to everyone else, like Karen-Green-the-Bean and Eeny-Meenie-Miny-Mo. Indeed, Angela by itself seemed foreshortened, for everyone knew that she had a string of names like a royal princess — Angela Mary Madeleva Elizabeth Vitale. The Elizabeth was for Enid's own mother, a circumstance which might have caused jealousy had not Angela been on a plane so far above the rest that envy or jealousy or rivalry was out of the question.

Karen Green's party unfolded exactly as Enid knew it would. After the games came a festival of gluttony, all that black-market sugar, hoarded butter, and borrowed trimmings could concoct. After that all the children, surfeited by too much starch and sugar, collapsed about the room. Some were tearful, some queasy, and some actually sick in the downstairs bathroom, while a grown-up banged on the door, saying, "Now you hurry up in there. Nigel needs to go very badly." All were overexcited—their dresses in disarray, spotted with trifle, jam, and every kind of nastiness, their ribbons fallen loose, and their hair tumbled about their faces. Then, as the fee exacted for the supposed pleasures, each was required to perform a party piece. Some tried to say poems and forgot the words; some banged on the piano, which was out of tune to begin with; and some sang "Early One Morning" and "As I Was Going to Strawberry Fair." A few hopeless cases refused to do anything and pleaded for Rennies and Beecham's Powders.

At last it was Angela's turn. She stood without hesitation among the casualties strewn about the floor like Napolean's Retreat From Moscow. The fire was banked up high, and some were flopped in front of it. The curtains were closed now and the lamps lit. When Angela stood up, a very tall girl, there was not the least strand of her hair escaped from its moorings, nor the slightest crumb on her velvet dress, nor the merest wrinkle in her white stockings. The lamplight illuminated her from behind like the picture of a saint. And when she began to sing, the pure sounds fell on the mob and so affected them that the snuffling ones hushed and fell into a kind of trance, as if a magic spell had subdued them.

And the song that Angela sang was always the same. It was one that Enid never heard anyone else sing on "Workers' Playtime" or "Housewives' Choice," although she listened for it constantly. Many of the songs were plaintive, and when her mother heard Vera Lynn singing "I'll be seeing you in all the old familiar places," she said, "It almost brings tears to your eyes." Enid agreed, but no song ever matched the ineffable sweetness and poignancy of Angela's, even though she could not understand the words. When she asked, Angela said, "It's the 'Ave Maria,' " and Enid understood that it was one of the songs that Angela learned at her convent school, which Enid sometimes visited when she stayed weekends and Angela's mother had them take a basket of bread to the nuns.

Enid herself went to a parish school with smelly lavatories and a horrid old headmaster with a drop on the end of his nose and a cane. He was no direct threat to Enid, but sometimes from behind the closed door of his room came sounds that filled her with dread and lacerated her senses—a whisk and a blow and a cry, all rising in sequence to a terrifying crescendo of whisks and blows and cries and stopping suddenly. Then out would creep an abject urchin with ragged clothes and a bloated face, shaking throughout his undernourished frame so much that he could barely walk. For Enid it was like living under the constant threat of violence and torture, and it cast a gloom over her days, like walking past the window of Madame Tussaud's—the hooded executioner, the nightmare torturer with the vulture's head.

It seemed entirely fitting that Angela should be spared such sights and sounds and live in a world of prayers, bell chimes, and silent nuns padding through cloisters. When they went together to the convent, they pulled a bell rope at the gate in the wall and stood waiting under the trees. Although they heard nothing when they rang, eventually an old nun with a gentle smile opened the big wooden gate and closed it after them. The nun led them inside, asking Angela, "And how is Lily-white today?" Everyone knew that Angela loved above all things (human) a pure white rabbit which she kept in a hutch in her garden. She visited this rabbit all the time and lifted her up, the rabbit nestling against Angela's cheek, laying back her white ears, and closing her eyes.

The nuns had a vegetable garden with a few dusty cabbages and onions and radishes, of which they were inordinately proud and watchful. They strung nets over the rows of sprouting greens "to thwart those thieving birds" and chased off the sheppies with extraordinary and un-nun-like rage. Angela, however, was allowed to go there and fill her basket with all the most tender and juicy leaves and take away whatever she wished for Lily-white. Greedily she pulled up the best lettuces and tenderest cabbages and put them in her basket while the nuns stood by, smiling encouragement.

The old nun took them indoors to where the place kept its deepest secrets. One on either side of her, they walked along the cloister, across the courtyard containing the statue of the Virgin Mary, and through the walled garden with the grotto and the water falling among ferns. And here it was that Angela went to school on weekdays and to chapel on Sundays, and learned the song that Enid thought was the most beautiful song in the world, the thought of which had made her quiver when Karen Green said to her, "Oh, and we've invited your Cousin Angela."

For days Enid had looked forward breathlessly to the song, and she was not disappointed. Angela stood, her face uplifted as in prayer, even the fingers that curled about the corner of the sofa back assuming an unconscious grace. "Ave Mari-i-i-a," began Angela in a soft and tentative voice. Then her voice gathered strength and grew louder, and notes floated on the air one after the other, the rhythm repeating itself, the voice seeming to caress the melody.

And even in the midst of her joy, it pained Enid just a little that this song was falling on the unworthy ears of all the dull-witted party-goers. When Angela sang in that caressing voice, Enid thought it was meant for her alone, and she could hardly bear that the notes were falling indiscriminately about the room so that all could overhear what she took to be a private message from Angela to herself.

For in spite of Angela's inaccessibility, her own life with her family and with the nuns, and her devotion to Lily-white, there was a part of her life that she shared only with Enid; it locked them together and drew a circle around them which no one else could enter. This shared secret bond had grown up during the long afternoons when their mothers drank tea and left the girls to play and keep out of mischief together.

The parents at this time, by their choice of playthings, propelled the girls forward toward the roles they would eventually fill. They gave them dollhouses, miniature cook stoves, and nurses' uniforms. Nursing during the war had assumed an important and romantic image. The newspapers and magazines regularly showed flocks of young women surrounding wounded soldiers and restoring and making them whole again. The children were given jigsaw puzzles which, when the last piece lay in place, revealed *The Lady with the Lamp*. They were given white aprons and simple headdresses with red crosses emblazoned on the front. Thus attired, they played for hours, bandaging broken toys, making splints and crutches, and placing bandages and poultices athwart the heads of ancient teddy bears.

In the severity of the nursing costume, Angela's beauty was heightened to a spectacular degree. The snood holding back her hair showed the elegance of her profile, the delicately curved nose, the wide expanse of brow. The grown-ups who long-sufferingly sat in for the bears and dolls were moved to make the joking compliments which Angela never failed to provoke and which, all the same, she never deigned to acknowledge with the merest shadow of a smile. Uncle Joe, known for his jokes, said, "Too beautiful for wards," and the other men said that if they were wounded, they hoped they'd be lucky enough to have a nurse like Angela "and then your Aunt Bertha wouldn't stand a chance." The aunts rolled their eyes and said, "Men!" and added more seriously that Angela wouldn't be a nurse for long after those clever young doctors saw her. And someone said, "Doctors, fiddlesticks! The Countess of Brinsley was a nurse before she got married. She was hired on private duty to nurse the old earl and look where she is now." And they sighed and smiled, for nothing seemed too good for Angela. It would not have surprised any of them to see Angela walking down the aisle of Westminster Abbey on the arm of an aged peer, and see the rest of the family welcomed and feted and received into what Enid's mother vaguely called *the best circles,* all because of their connection with the beauteous Angela.

And when at last the toys lost their appeal and no grown-ups were forthcoming, Enid and Angela improvised by ministering to each other. Replacing bears and uncles, each allowed the other to apply bandages and set broken limbs in splints. And it was from this blameless pastime that their play took a turn that was no longer quite so innocent. Angela, in her guise as nurse, introduced an element which was not at all lady-like and which at first bothered Enid. She was by nature fearful, and the game now demanded the utmost privacy. It could only be played in the secrecy of a tent or in a distant corner of attic, shrubbery, or gazebo. Even there the danger was great that some grown-up might surprise them or that little Johnny might creep up on them and run off screaming, "I'm telling, I'm telling," though what he would have told or understood seems hard to imagine, the new part of the nursing game having no place in the vocabulary of the children, or the grown-ups either for that matter. But Enid's unease had another source. During this game, a terrifying transformation came over Angela. Her face ceased to be serene and spiritual, and turned into a mask of sensuality, so that Enid, opening her eyes, would see Angela watching her with a terrifying, inhuman smile that was not friendly but more like the grimace of a panting dog. And in his one game Angela was not her gentle self, but rough, insistent, and tireless. Once on a lazy Sunday afternoon, when they met at the house of their shared grandmother, Angela took Enid aside and whispered, "Let's play nurses." Enid had replied, "But we don't have our outfits," before she realized that the phrase was simply a form of shorthand. Thereafter, the trappings of the game — the splints, the bandages, the headdresses with the red cross emblazoned on them — were tossed aside and only the one essential element remained, that which needed merely secrecy and silence and the hidden corners of the house and garden.

For all its terrors, it was this game which bound together Enid and her Cousin Angela and which caused Enid to look forward tremblingly to the moment when Angela should stand up at the party and sing the song, which now seemed like an anthem to their union and to the bond between them that was as strong as the ties of family or faith.

When Angela began to sing, her voice was at first hesitant, but it steadied and gathered force. The notes strengthened and grew louder — "Ave Mar-ii-ii-a." The words and the rhythms repeated themselves, and love flowed into the song as Angela's voice caressed the words and caressed the ears of Enid, listening in a kind of rapture. Angela closed her eyes, and her face assumed an expression so tender and ethereal that she looked like an angel of God. Then after the melody and volume had swelled, it curled in upon itself again and fell away into a hush, and the notes vibrated long after they finished. But in the middle there was a corridor of the song in which Angela's voice mellowed and matched the words. "Sant-a Mar-i-i-i-a" came like a plea for help, unbearably drawn out in a beseeching, tormented cry. In this corridor in the middle of the song Enid's excitement reached a peak of intensity, and her heart almost stopped in a moment of pure and uplifting ecstasy. When it was over, she was left spent and ready to burst into tears, as if she had been drowned and drowned again. But after that, what then?

How skittish a colt is memory in its leaps about the meadow of the past. Now it stops, open-eyed and wary, in a clear patch of light, alert to every passing breeze, snapping at a dragonfly. Now it notices every delicate tracery in the petals of the water lilies on the castle moat. Then again, for months and years on end it lies soporific in clover like an old brewer's dray put out to grass, mind dulled, senses deadened, resistant to any effort to budge and prod it to its feet. How Enid tried to remember. There in the clear light, fresh as the day it happened, was the image of Angela, preserved like a flower crystallized in ice, singing "Ave Maria." Yet on either side of that moment were the accumulated days and weeks and months that no trick or blandishment could persuade memory to yield again. Out of this chaos came Angela's face like a disembodied spirit, saying dread words: *"Lily-white died last week and we buried her in the convent garden," "I'm going to be a nun," "I shan't play with you anymore."* But when and where they were spoken and how inflected, Enid could not recall. Did Angela say "I shan't play with *you*" or "I shan't *play* anymore" or "*I* shan't play with you"? Oh memory, thought Enid, get up, old horse, but it never did. All she remembered subsequently had only the most tenuous connection with her Cousin Angela and her singing at the party given to celebrate the birthday of Karen Green.

At the end of the party, the children were bustled into scarves and mittens and wellies and given a small gift to carry home. Enid, who had journeyed the farthest, was taken out by Karen Green's father to be put on the bus, which was to be met three stops down the road by her own father. It was a drizzling, foggy night and she stood waiting under the gas lamp which served the double function of street light and sign post for the bus stop. When the lamps had been first introduced into the village, one faction had opposed them on the grounds that they were sacrilegious since God had provided the moon to help those who issued forth at night. But on this night there was no moon, only the gas lamp and many brown-winged moths destroying themselves in its pale light and heat. Enid stood in the penumbra, which was exactly like the one she could see when she sat up in bed, lifted her bedroom curtain, and peered at the bus stop across the street from her house.

After a while, a man with a turned-up collar stepped out from the shadows. "Supposed to come at ten past, is it?" he asked. "Ten past and twenty to the hour," replied Tracy Green absently. The man said, "Live in these parts, do you?" Tracy, alert now, looked at him warily and said, "Aye. I have the tailoring business down the street, and you?" "On compassionate leave," said the man. "I go back tomorrow. Maybe when it's all over I'll let you measure me up for a suit. If I'm still alive." "Be glad to," said Tracy, but in an uncomfortable voice. "That your little lass?" asked the man. "No," said Tracy, "I'm putting her on the bus, and her dad's meeting her at the other end." "Tell you what," said the man. "How about me buying you a drink in yon pub when you've got rid of the lass." But at that moment the bus came along, and Tracy got on, mumbling to Enid that he'd best see her all the way home. When they got off, Enid's father was waiting at the bus stop. He said, "Why Trace, you didn't have to come all the way." "Well, you never know," said Karen Green's father. "There's some rum folk about these days and anyway I need a bit of a walk," and he sprinted quickly away into the rain.

As Enid sat by the fire drinking warm milk, her mother placed an outstretched palm on her brow and said, "I sometimes wonder about these parties. They get them all het up." Her father said, "That's true, but they need something to look forward to in times like these." Enid thought about the party and about the man with the upturned collar who was going back to the war and perhaps to death. She had the feeling that something very sinister had been averted. But what it was and from whom it was averted, she had no means of knowing.

Years later, long after she had lost faith in her memory and its ability to bear trustworthy witness to anything, she asked her mother, "So when did the Vitales finally leave?" Her mother was garrulous and unreliable in her old age, but Enid always hoped (and at the same time dreaded) that her questions might surprise a revelation. "You ask that every time you come over," said her mother. "It was after the war and just before my sister died. What was her name?"

"Nancy, Mother. Your Nancy."

"Yes, our Nan. And your Cousin Angela went into a convent. What a waste. She could have had anybody she wanted. I think of her when I see these actresses. Not one a patch on Angela. What's that one with the foolish name?" "Twiggy, Mother." (Enid had long since ceased to be offended by the assumption that she remained single because she had no choice in the matter.)

"Yes, stupid nonsense and waste. Wicked. And little Johnny too. They got him as well. 'Father', they call him now. And they changed her name. What do they call her?"

"Sister Mary Magdalene."

"My sister's only girl and my own namesake and never a word from that day to this. They don't allow them any contact with *the outside world.*

"Mother, that's not true . . ."

"It is. And they shave their heads. That beautiful dark hair. . . ." Her mother set off on a trail of baseless grudges and recriminations as circuitous and irrelevant as Enid's own, but no scent ever led exactly to where Enid hoped (and feared) or told her what she wished (and was afraid) to remember. Sometimes it seemed to Enid that she had spent her whole life in a vain effort to retrieve that lost time and to recapture the peak of joy she had reached when her Cousin Angela had stood up among the disorderly array of children and sung — for her alone — "Ave Maria."

For this reason, on a wet autumn evening in a cold northern city on another continent, where she lectured to students on Women in Medieval Society, Enid set out again. She hoped to secure one of the last-minute seats (as always the birthday had taken her by surprise) at a concert by a celebrated young cellist. The musician was an eighteen-year-old girl whose youth and beauty and artistry had already elicited a cult following of those inclined to hero worship. The hall was crowded with devotees, but Enid managed to find a seat, and for two hours she sat spellbound while the young virtuoso rendered piece after piece, to the mounting excitement of her fans. As she played, the cellist closed her eyes, shut her face, and retreated into a world to which she admitted no one. And when at last she was forced to acknowledge the frenzied applause of her admirers, she did so with a bewildered look on her face, like one awakened from a deep trance. The audience, keyed up to an incredible pitch of excitement, brayed for encore after encore. "Bravo!" they cried, "bravo!" But Enid, slightly repelled by this public display of near hysteria, slipped off into the moonless night. For nothing in her adult life would ever approach the rapturous sense of beauty and energy and ecstasy that she had felt years ago on this same day in that magical moment at the birthday party of the unspeakable Karen Green.

Back in her rooms at the college, she was unable to compose herself for sleep. Rising from her bed, she turned on the lamp by the armchair in which she always sat to read. She took from its shelf her volume of *The Complete Works of Geoffrey Chaucer.* She opened it where the marker lay in the Prologue to *The Canterbury Tales.* And she read again, as she had times without number, the description of Madame Eglentyne, the prioress.

The Decline and Fall
of a Reasonable Woman

Each year when she returned home for the summer, Sibyl studied her parents closely for signs of change. She noticed, however, that they did not so much change as intensify. They were becoming not shadows of their former selves but more substantial versions. At times, even caricatures.

Was this, she wondered, the result of their living in Poynings-on-Sea. The town, a mecca for retired people, had in its earlier days drawn its population from the veterans of the Indian Army. She speculated that the majors and colonels, returning from lives of anarchic freedom in exotic places, had been only too thankful to lapse into rigid patterns of conventionality. Once established, these patterns had remained unchanged even when the majors and colonels gave way to veterans of provincial banks and London stock-brokerage firms. At least, this was the theory by which she accounted for the fixity of life in Poynings-on-Sea, where the people, no matter how they had lived elsewhere, moved with the sedate and decorous movements of minuet dancers, through four phases of being.

They began in the formal dignity of The Big House, a sturdy edifice in its own grounds, surrounded by shaven lawns, trim flower beds, and stone urns triumphantly ablaze with geraniums. On a highly polished plate on the front gate was emblazoned the name of the estate: High Cedars, Green Meadows, Twin Oaks, or Three Chimneys.

In the next phase, The Bungalow, it was necessary to make retrenchments. Certain problems loomed: The Garden, The Difficulty of Finding Help, or some insidious natural phenomenon like The Rising Damp — so a move was made to a small square bungalow with a diminished garden. Bravely the bungalow-dwellers clung to their dignity. The urns of geraniums assumed greater prominence against the reduced scale of the entrance. The names on the gates had a certain defiance: Runnymeade, Glamis, Tara, and Elsinore. Never a day passed without the owners congratulating each other on the wisdom of the move and the convenience of their present circumstances.

Alas, the problems were only in abeyance. After some years they loomed again. The help proved elusive, the garden became Too Much, and the damp started to rise again. The time had come to abandon the bungalow, the nameplate, and the urns, and to make the transition to The Seafront Flat. Even here, in somewhat cramped conditions, life retained its dignity. The post brought letters addressed to the Kensington Suite, Charters Towers, and Cambridge Mansions. The geraniums, now in wooden boxes, bowed their heads bravely before the salt breezes of the English Channel. A liveried doorkeeper, who was kindness itself, commended himself by his deftness in retrieving scattered packages and in steering unsteady legs from the front door to the lift. Their diminished senses unoffended by the odors of bacon and chips and onions that seeped under their doors, the flat-dwellers congratulated themselves daily on their liberation from the tyranny of sweeping paths, polishing knockers, and shaking out doormats.

These three transformations Sibyl could contemplate with perfect equanimity. Her parents were at the bungaloid stage, and she knew that in the fullness of time the transition to The Seafront Flat would be effected as smoothly as the earlier one from The Big House to The Bungalow. It was the final transition at which she balked. Its very neatness and simplicity seemed an affront to reason.

She noted that in every part of the world people showed commendable variety and originality in the causes of their deaths. They fell victim to accidents, operations, violent criminal assaults, or diseases. They disappeared in a flurry of invading daughters-in-law, surrounded by white-coated medical practitioners or attended by gentlemen of the cloth. It defied reason that in Poynings-on-Sea alone in the whole civilized world, these eventualities did not occur. The natives dropped cleanly in their tracks. They passed away in their sleep, drew their last breaths while watching the late-night news on the telly, or dropped at the age of ninety-two in telephone booths.

Sibyl often tried to settle the matter with her father. Doing so was not easy since he did not argue or converse but communicated chiefly by means of Utterances. He listened to what was spoken, drew on his pipe, and eventually made pronouncements that floated out, oracular and final, like banner headlines that immediately assume the permanence of the eternal verities—Your Country Needs You, Go West, Young Man, or Guinness Is Good for You.

Having uttered, he refused to be drawn out further and withdrew behind a screen of pipe smoke. The Great Oz had spoken. Not only were his Utterances unarguable, but they were restricted in number so that by sparseness and repetition they gained weight and significance. When questioned about the demise of a friend, his utterance was invariable and talismanic. There was only one single reason, ever: His ticker stopped.

Sibyl, a professor of philosophy in a small college in western Canada, was trained in logic and practiced in argument. She could not brook this assault on logic. She protested it vociferously, growing pink in the face and — she was no longer young — feeling the dewlaps that had developed in her neck and that wobbled alarmingly when she was angry.

"Look here, Daddy." (She was one of those middle-aged Englishwomen who still called her parents Mummy and Daddy.) "There are millions of things that people die of." She counted them off on her fingers—Crone's disease, Houghton's syndrome, Paget's disease, Sherman's disease, Parkinson's disease, dozens to choose from. She invoked the Medical Dictionary, the obituary columns in *The Daily Telegraph,* the crimes reported in *The News of the World,* and *The Book of Martyrs.* Nothing could shake his blind faith in the Grim Reaper as a watchmaker. Moreover, every summer it seemed his point of view was confirmed, hers refuted. Breakfasts, luncheons, mid-morning coffees, afternoon teas, cocktail hours, and dinner parties were ruined for her by one recurrent conversation.

"Heard in the Devonshire that Old Gebbie died."

"What'd he die of?" Sibyl asked sharply.

Her father puffed his pipe, swirled his wine in his glass or stirred his tea, and uttered: "TICKER STOPPED."

Complete triumph of unreason.

Sibyl wanted to crash her hand down on the table and make all the teacups dance in the air, but she was a reasonable woman and controlled herself. She tried instead, as a kind of academic exercise, to find some logic in the foggy workings of her father's mind. There were, subsequent upon the ticker-stopping, two corollary comments. These were: CAN'T GO ON FOREVER, YOU KNOW and HE WAS NO AGE AT ALL. Sometimes one applied and sometimes the other. Sibyl tried to determine the rules of usage.

Every morning, like the rest of the local population, Sibyl read *The Poynings Observer*. It was a Poynings joke that the inhabitants turned first to the obituary section, and if they didn't find their own names there, got up. Sibyl also turned first to the obituaries. It amused her to read the messages about and to the deceased. She discovered that whole segments of the community believed that their loved ones still subscribed to, or at least read, *The Poynings Observer*. They printed messages of affection and grief and, sometimes, veiled threats:

> About a thousand little things,
> You used to say I nagged.
> Not long the respite that Death brings,
> Though I behind have lagged.
>
> You thought to leave me far behind
> And seek a better place;
> Think not that you have seen the last
> Of my familiar face.

While she savored the verses and the Cooper's Oxford marmalade, Sibyl tested her father's Utterances:

"I see where old Waddington died, age eighty-two."

"CAN'T GO ON FOREVER, YOU KNOW."

"I see where Cicily Leatherborrow died at seventy-three."

"NO AGE AT ALL REALLY."

"I see where. . . ."

"NO AGE. . . ."

"I see where. . . ."

"CAN'T GO. . . ."

"I see where Herbert Laithwaite died at seventy-nine. . . . No age?"

"CAN'T GO ON FOR . . ." (furiously and amid a shower of toast crumbs).

Thus, Sibyl established the cut-off date with exactitude at eighty.

Her mother, easier to engage and defeat in conversation than her father, took no part in these exchanges unless the obituary notice included the phrase NO FLOWERS BY REQUEST. She was an impassioned gardener, a boon companion to every florist and nurseryman in the town, and the moratorium on flowers incensed her.

"It's all very well for people to have self-righteous notions about sending money to homes for stray cats and saving horses from being eaten in France, but what about the flower shops? I was talking to Leonard Greengrass, and business is very bad at the moment. People are so short-sighted and shallow in their thinking."

Sibyl relished the chance to refute such an argument.

"Ah, but Mummy, if you follow that line of reasoning, you'd be sending boxes of sweets and boxes of kippers. Think of the toffee shops, think of the poor hardworking fishmongers."

Triumph of reason. She smiled slyly and inwardly at her own agility of mind.

"Well, kippers come from the Isle of Man at this time of year," replied her mother. "I was thinking more of our local merchants. I like that crystallized ginger you got, Sibyl dear. Get some more when next you go into town."

Reason did not have an easy time triumphing in Poynings-on-Sea.

The same spareness and severity of line that governed her parents' world view also governed their social life. Here the donnée was that they were too set in their ways to relish spending the evening in someone else's house, eating someone else's food, or drinking someone else's wines and spirits. But working against this principle was the fact that they were naturally friendly and interested in people. Her father dropped into the Devonshire for a preprandial drink, her mother went to bring-and-buy sales. They struck up friendships and invitations ensued. Since her parents were infallibly polite, they accepted. After one uncomfortable evening the visits were discontinued on grounds expressed tersely by her father and documented by her mother: THE DOG ("a nasty great brute of a thing"), THE SHERRY ("very nasty treacly stuff, could hardly force it down"), THE HOUSE ("nasty barn of a place, causes rheumatism I shouldn't wonder"). All subsequent invitations would be refused with the blanket excuse that the night air didn't suit her mother. Her father, of course, had been against the visit from the start, and had been inveigled into it only on the grounds that the man of the house fell into one of his vague categories of approval: HIS HEART WAS IN THE RIGHT PLACE, HE WOULD GIVE YOU THE SHIRT OFF HIS BACK or HIS LAST PENNY, or her father had known him for twenty years and he was ALWAYS THE SAME.

Politely, the invitation would be extended in the opposite direction, but the one-sided nature of the visiting soon rankled, and the pronouncement that IT WAS ALL ONE-WAY TRAFFIC became the epitaph for another dead friendship.

Sibyl had noted for some years the surprising longevity of her parents' friendship with the Fortescue-Foulkeses and had presumed that Old Forty's sameness and generous instincts as to his shirt and last penny had not been tarnished by the nastiness of the dog, the sherry, and the house. Her mother had braved the night air, and one-way traffic had continued cheerfully in the reverse direction.

Therefore, when her mother had dropped hints all summer long about Winifred Fortescue-Foulkes's desire to meet her, Sibyl was inclined, in the spirit of intellectual curiosity, to spend an evening with them. This curiosity was sharpened considerably when, en route to the Fortescue-Foulkeses' house, her parents started an ominous duet of warnings.

"You know there's nothing at all wrong with Winifred, Sibyl dear."

"HEART IN THE RIGHT PLACE."

"And Forty is very pleasant when you get to know him."

"Old Forty? Known him twenty years. ALWAYS THE SAME, OLD FORTY."

"A most friendly couple. . . ."

"GIVE YOU. . . ."

"ALWAYS. . . ."

"THE RIGHT PLACE. . . ."

It emerged that Winifred's most noticeable quirk was her habit of calling people by the names she thought they should have, rather than by the names they really had. Forty's real name was Robin, but she called him Clarence. Sibyl's father's name was Henry, but she called him Malcolm. When she shook hands with Sibyl, she said, "I've so longed to meet you, Rosemary."

All this was not nearly so illogical as it seemed. There was nothing bright or chirpy about Forty, and even Sibyl had to admit that he was more Clarence than Robin. Of extremely advanced age (Sibyl guessed in his late nineties) and paralyzed by strokes, he was a mere shrunken huddle of clothes in a wheelchair. His lugubrious face registered no recognizable expression. His heart might have been in the right place, but the question of his offering the shirt off his back was moot. He was entirely speechless.

On close inspection the grounds of the long friendship still remained puzzling. The house was the epitome of a great, drafty barn, the sherry was the last word in awfulness, and on top of everything else, there was a huge, slobbering mastiff with halitosis. The dog was called Fido. Or perhaps, Sibyl thought, Phaedo.

Clearly, there was a great deal more to the FF's than appeared on the surface. Their hearts, whether in the right places or not, must have been formidably tough. Under their bland faces they must have concealed wills of iron. Their remaining in such a place at their advanced age was testimony to amazing tenacity, for the house was a monument to their defiance of all the Poynings proprieties. The front gate, which bore the cryptic sign CARVEN, was sunk so deep into the ground that visitors were compelled to enter through a hole in the hedge. From the urns straggled ivied creepers, having long ago strangled the geraniums. On the lawns dandelions were rampant. In the flower beds lilies-of-the-valley were festering and smelling far worse than weeds. At the back of the house monkey-puzzle trees leaned about crazily, and on a little knoll lurched the cockeyed remains of a wooden gazebo. Peering through the diamond-shaped windowpanes, Sibyl could see imaginary toads and iguanas lurking in the shrubbery.

The conversation was as cockeyed as the gazebo.

"How do you like A-merri-cah?" asked Winifred.

"I live in Canada, actually."

"Everywhere is very far apart there, isn't it?"

"Those wide open spices," said her father in his wild approximation of an American accent.

"I spoke once with a lady whose son-in-law was a lorry driver in Orr-i-gone," said her mother.

"Clarence was in Florr-i-dah as a young man. We exchanged Christmas cards for years with a very nice lady there."

"I'm so thankful that Sibyl didn't get an A-merri-can accent. That was what I most dreaded when she went to live abroad," said her mother.

"I heard on the wireless the other day. . . ."

Sibyl wanted to ask what took Forty to Florida, but she couldn't decide whether she should refer to him as Robin, Clarence, or Forty. She was getting quite light-headed from the sherry and the surfeit of non sequiturs. She even forgot to wonder why, in this of all years, Winifred was so eager to meet her.

She did not, in fact, find out until six months after she had returned to Canada and forgotten the strange evening with the Fortescue-Foulkeses. She knew well the kind of thing that Poynings-dwellers asked of her. They were usually commissions that sounded easy but that were outrageously inconvenient: "Sibyl dear, you write so well. Would you write for me. . . ?" or "Sibyl, Mother said you go up to town sometimes. Would you bring me from Harrod's. . . ?"

Even by Poynings's standards Winifred's letter was dazzling in its gall. Sibyl had learned, soon after she left England, that Forty had died. Apparently, he had died as he had lived, defying all the established rules of conduct for Poynings-on-Sea. Her father took the unprecedented move of stating the cause of death: A MASSIVE CARDIAC

ARREST. Sibyl had a fleeting image of someone taking a sledgehammer to Big Ben. The letter arrived two months later.

Dear Rosemary,

I am so happy that I had the pleasure of meeting you last summer. You will have heard of my great loss. Your dear mother has been such a comfort to me in my distress. She told me that you offered to do anything you could to help. I am therefore taking the liberty of making a small request.

Would you be kind enough to scatter in Newfoundland the small box of ashes which I have received from the crematorium. My late husband would have wished this. I am deeply grateful and hope that I shall have the pleasure of seeing you when next you are in Poynings-on-Sea.

Yours sincerely,
Clarissa Fortescue-Foulkes

Since no ashes were included, Sibyl postponed her fury and thought that perhaps someone would reason with Winifred on the subject of distances, plane fares, and hotel bills. She hoped that she had heard the last of the matter, but this was not to be. The box arrived in her Christmas package from home, along with a Liberty silk scarf, a round tin box containing a Christmas cake, and a small Christmas pudding, packaged in red cellophane, with a sprig of plastic holly on top. Sibyl immediately threw out the pudding and the Christmas cake. She realized that it was wasteful and irrational to throw out the cake, but she could not bring herself to eat something that had been in transit for three weeks with the remains of Forty. She thought of him hunched and speechless in his wheelchair and felt nauseated. She had, of course, no intention of taking him to Newfoundland and she set him aside temporarily. Shelving him was not easy. During the academic year Sibyl occupied rooms in one of the college halls of residence. She had a spacious apartment with a large living/dining room, a study, a bedroom, a kitchen, and a bathroom. The problem was that there was no obvious place for Forty. It seemed insulting to his memory to put him in the medicine chest in the bathroom, and equally irreverent to place him next to the tinned goods on the kitchen shelves. She definitely did not want him in her bedroom, and when she put him in a bureau drawer, she kept feeling compelled to leave it open so that he could get some air. Never had

she felt so acutely the lack of a mantlepiece, the only really appropriate place in a home for a person's remains. Eventually, she left
him about the living room, now on a coffee table, now on a book-
shelf. The problem with this arrangement was that casual visitors
tended absentmindedly to pick up the box and toy with Forty while
they were talking or sipping martinis. Also, on days when the place
was cleaned, she was as nervous as a kitten and left a large sign:
PLEASE DO NOT THROW OUT. Finally, she started to carry him in her
briefcase to her office.

She did her level best to forget about him, but circumstances con-
spired constantly to remind her. "Life begins at forty," someone announced, and she jumped violently. In the grocery store she was
waiting patiently for the clerk to check out her purchases, and when
the girl said, "$40.75," Sibyl was so shocked that she dropped a jar of
pickled onions. At a faculty cocktail party the Dean leaned over and
said to her confidentially, "I have to confess, Sibyl, that on Sunday
afternoons I usually take forty winks." She started so suddenly that
she spilled her drink on his immaculate Brooks Brothers suit and
caused a sensation. After that people started to ask her very pointed-
ly how she was as if they really wished to know.

The situation worsened with the onset of Lent. Many of her students appeared in class on Ash Wednesday with smears of ash on
their faces, and she felt momentarily alarmed for the safety of Forty.
Once she went to read in the library of one of the affiliated religious
colleges, and as she sat there, voices drifted up from the chapel:

Forty days and forty nights,
We were wandering in the wild. . . .
Forty. . . forty. . . .

She left her books and bolted. It was monstrous, monstrous. She
thought that the winter blizzards spoke and reminded her, that the
wind accused her, and that the organ in the chapel and the thunder in
the air all pronounced the name of Forty.

The young biology professor from Yorkshire who occupied the
rooms next to Sibyl in residence often gave noisy parties. She had
long ago decided against Getting Into It with the neighbors, and during his bacchanalia she calmly switched on her light, made a thermos

of lemon tea, and, like the reasonable woman she was, read Plato. But now that she had Forty in the apartment, she was upset by the rowdy choruses of "On Ilkley Moor Bah't 'at." By the end of the song, "Thee will catch thee death of cold. . . . Worms will cum and eat thee up," she was shivering all over. When at last she slept, she had a terrifying dream, full of odd reverberations and strange chains of association. She dreamed of Winifred taking a great croquet mallet and shattering Forty into smithereens, and of Fido and the Canada geese by the lake eating all the shattered fragments. The next morning she was weak and shaky and much too exhausted to teach her classes. She felt as if tentacles of unreason were reaching out from Poynings and clutching at the very roots of her sanity.

"I am getting A Thing about Forty," she told herself.

As soon as she had articulated that fact, she determined to act without delay and put an end to what she now called, in order to put it into proper perspective, "This Ridiculous Forty Pantomime."

Once the decision was made, it was fairly easy to carry out. The Canadian Philosophical Association was meeting in St. John's, and without pausing to raise the fare from the Canada Council, she booked a flight to eastern Canada. It was plain sailing from that moment. She flew to St. John's and checked into the Sheraton Hotel in the early afternoon of a bright spring day. The only hitch was that she had to stay an extra day because she had overlooked the fact that it was April 1. She felt she could not tell Winifred that she had scattered Forty on All Fools' Day. On the second day of the month, therefore, she carried Forty to a nearby park, opened the box, and let the contents fall about a colorful herbaceous border. She could not help feeling that it was a whole lot neater than the garden he was used to at home. She did not attend any of the papers at the conference because her powers of concentration had been severely impaired by the emotional turmoil of the previous months. Her last act before leaving St. John's was to send a telegram to Winifred. It read:

MAJOR FORTESCUE-FOULKES LAID TO REST IN NEWFOUNDLAND.

After sending it off, she boarded the DC 10 for home.

"It is finished," she told herself.

But it wasn't. The last act in The Ridiculous Pantomime came soon after she arrived in Poynings for the summer. She was having breakfast with her parents on a cloudless July morning. For days the conversation had been taken up with the fierce equinoctial gales which had struck the town in the previous spring. The promenade had been pounded by huge waves. Beach huts had been demolished, lifeboats destroyed, lives lost, imaginations boggled, and rhetoric beggared. Her mother could hardly bear the thought that Sibyl had missed it all. "It was the worst storm in living memory," she said. "I was so thankful you weren't here at such a terrible time. The Wraigs lost their beach cottage and the nice man who sold them fish for the last twenty years."

"This ginger marmalade is simply lovely," she added. "Pick up some more when you go into town."

"And you might pop into the cemetery and see the grave where Forty's buried," her father said. "Winifred would appreciate your interest."

There was something about the conjunction of Forty's grave and Winifred's appreciation that set off an internal fire alarm somewhere deep in Sibyl's consciousness. She very deliberately set down her cup in its flowered saucer and said quietly, "How could he be buried in Poynings when I scattered his remains in Newfoundland?"

It took her parents some minutes to digest the question and then they spoke in a single voice: "Not Forty's ashes, Fido's."

"Oh, Sibyl," her mother said, "you didn't really think . . . ? You do get some odd notions. I sometimes think it comes from living abroad. Winifred told me she got a very odd message from you."

"But why the dog?" asked Sibyl. "*It* hadn't been to Newfoundland, surely."

"Well, it was a Newfoundland hound," explained her mother, "and Winifred thought it would be appropriate. She so appreciated your help."

"Thought The World of that dog," said her father.

"More than she did of Forty, some people thought," said her mother.

"Oh, there's nothing wrong with Winifred really," said her father.

"HEART IN THE RIGHT PLACE," said her mother.

Sibyl touched her dewlaps very gingerly and remembered a conversation she had had with her brother on one of his infrequent visits. Neville was a bank manager in Tunbridge Wells, and Sibyl thought he was the most conventional and narrow-minded person she had ever known. She also thought he was negligent in his attentions to their parents.

"You should come down more often," she'd scolded him. "It isn't all that far and they would appreciate it."

"To tell you the truth, Sibby," he'd replied, "I often think it isn't a good thing for you to spend as much time as you do with them. Months on end. You could get like them."

"You mean," she said, "a bit cuckoo?"

"I mean stark, raving bonkers," he said.

"Well, his words had proved prophetic. She could now see quite clearly that it had happened. The events of the last six months had shown that. She had become enmeshed beyond all reason in their strange machinations. But fortunately it was not too late. Once again, as when she had decided to put an end to her preoccupation with the ashes of Forty, or Fido rather, she took stock of the situation and determined to extricate herself immediately.

"I have been thinking," she said. "I am underfoot here. Next year I shall get a flat on the seafront for the summer."

They digested this statement for a time, chewing silently.

"Not a flat at your age," her father said at last.

"You should get a house, Sibyl," her mother said. "The place would then be ready for you when you retire. Everyone would give you clippings for the garden. You wouldn't need to buy a single plant except for the larger shrubs. If I were you, I'd get a cat. So much less trouble than a dog, and you might find a nice ginger Tom."

"Old Brodgen's the best estate agent in town," said her father.

"Winifred put her house on the market just last week," said her mother. "The garden would need a lot of work, but I believe the price is quite likely to be within reason."

There was a pause, and her parents looked across the table at each other and smiled. A single thought shaped itself in the air above their heads and formed a banner headline, inevitable, indisputable, irrevocable: IT WAS MEANT TO BE. Sibyl received the utterance like a decree from a higher power. She felt as if something she had been pulling against for eons of time had suddenly been removed. All the resistance had fallen away, and in its place was a beautiful, calm acceptance. She surrendered her will easily, peacefully. Blissfully she contemplated her future. Brogden would find her a house. Everything would fall into place. Decisions would be made without anguish, without surprise, one thing leading naturally to another, with no more confusion, turmoil, or argument. There would be all the time in the world. And in the meantime, she helped herself to another spoonful of marmalade and pushed her teacup toward the teapot, sitting snug under its little furry busby.

ILLINOIS SHORT FICTION